X ack

Dunwich
Pt Lookout
Amity Pt
Russell Island
~~Macleay Island~~ 3/16
Mobile Library

cir
Guidins

H

Slaughter Canyon

**Center Point
Large Print**

Also by Joseph A. West and available from Center Point Large Print:

The Burning Range
The Last Manhunt
The Stranger from Abilene
The Ghost of Apache Creek

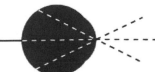

**This Large Print Book carries the
Seal of Approval of N.A.V.H.**

Ralph Compton

Slaughter Canyon

A Ralph Compton Novel
by Joseph A. West

CENTER POINT LARGE PRINT
THORNDIKE, MAINE

This Center Point Large Print edition
is published in the year 2012 by arrangement with
NAL Signet, a member of Penguin Group (USA) Inc.

This is a work of fiction. Names, characters,
places, and incidents either are the product of
the author's imagination or are used fictitiously,
and any resemblance to actual persons,
living or dead, business establishments, events,
or locales is entirely coincidental.

The text of this Large Print edition is unabridged.
In other aspects, this book may vary
from the original edition.
Printed in the United States of America
on permanent paper.
Set in 16-point Times New Roman type.

ISBN: 978-1-61173-459-1

Library of Congress Cataloging-in-Publication Data

West, Joseph A.
Slaughter canyon : a Ralph Compton novel / Joseph A. West and Ralph
Compton. — Large print ed.
    p. cm. — (Center Point large print edition)
ISBN 978-1-61173-459-1 (library binding : alk. paper)
1. Large type books. I. Compton, Ralph. II. Title.
PS3573.E8224S53 2012
813′.54—dc23
                                                              2012008674

THE IMMORTAL COWBOY

This is respectfully dedicated to the "American Cowboy." His was the saga sparked by the turmoil that followed the Civil War, and the passing of more than a century has by no means diminished the flame.

True, the old days and the old ways are but treasured memories, and the old trails have grown dim with the ravages of time, but the spirit of the cowboy lives on.

In my travels—to Texas, Oklahoma, Kansas, Nebraska, Colorado, Wyoming, New Mexico, and Arizona—I always find something that reminds me of the Old West. While I am walking these plains and mountains for the first time, there is this feeling that a part of me is eternal, that I have known these old trails before. I believe it is the undying spirit of the frontier calling me, through the mind's eye, to step back into time. What is the appeal of the Old West of the American frontier?

It has been epitomized by some as the dark and bloody period in American history. Its heroes—Crockett, Bowie, Hickok, Earp—have been reviled and criticized. Yet the Old West lives on, larger than life.

It has become a symbol of freedom, when there was always another mountain to climb and another river to cross; when a dispute between two men was settled not with expensive lawyers, but with fists, knives, or guns. Barbaric? Maybe. But some things never change. When the cowboy rode into the pages of American history, he left behind a legacy that lives within the hearts of us all.

—Ralph Compton

Chapter 1

A Challenge in the Night

Deputy U.S. Marshal Matt Battles sat his horse and studied the rain-lashed railroad siding. Under his slicker, his right hand rested on the worn walnut handle of the Colt tucked into his waistband.

A man born to vigilance, Battles's hard, clear blue eyes scanned the railroad car drawn up just a few feet from the end of the rails. A chuffing locomotive made up the rest of the train, there being no other cars but the big Pullman.

Four soldiers wearing rubberized ponchos stood guard outside the car, their bayoneted rifles gleaming in the downpour. One smoked a pipe, his hand over the glowing coal to keep it alight.

Battles shifted in the saddle and then winced as pain gnawed at his left thigh. Carson City Tom Sanchez had put lead in there three years before. It had not been a serious wound as wounds go, but a hurt like that does pain a man in rainy weather.

Battles lifted his head as lightning scrawled across the night sky and thunder rumbled, still distant, but coming his way.

"Well, Matt," he said aloud, the habit of men

who ride lonely trails, "let's get the damned thing over with."

He kneed his buckskin forward and rode down a shallow, grassy rise to the gravel flat beside the tracks.

The sudden appearance of a tall man riding a stud horse drew an immediate response from the soldiers.

"Halt! Who goes there?" the smoking man challenged, talking through teeth clenched on the pipe stem.

Battles drew rein, then said his name.

The soldier's proper response should've been "Pass, friend, and be recognized."

It wasn't.

"Come in slow and keep your hands where I can see them," the soldier said. "I got faith in this here Springfield."

Battles rode to within three feet of the soldiers and stopped. They faced him in a bayoneted semicircle, neither hostile nor friendly, just ready and aware.

The four men had the lean, tough look of old Apache fighters and had probably been hand-picked for this guard detail.

A careful man himself, the marshal kept his motions to a minimum and none of them were quick.

"State your intentions," the pipe-smoking soldier said.

Battles's amused smile erased a dozen years from his face and softened the hard, tight planes of his jaw and mouth.

"My intention is to follow my orders and present myself to the president of the United States," he said. Then, as a clincher: "I have a letter of introduction from Governor Roberts."

"Wait there," the soldier said. "I'll talk to the colonel."

He vanished inside the Pullman and appeared a few moments later, followed by a beautiful officer wearing an impeccable dress uniform, gleaming in blue, silver, and gold. A black spade-shaped beard, trimmed, combed, and scented, spread across his breast and he wore a crested signet ring on his left pinky finger.

The officer stayed under the shelter of the car's platform and beckoned Battles closer. He stretched out an arm and was visibly irritated as raindrops spattered his uniform.

"I'm Colonel James Sinclair," he said. "Show me your bona fides."

Battles reached under his slicker, a move that tensed the soldiers, and produced two pieces of paper. One he passed to the colonel, the other he again stuffed under his slicker.

As Sinclair read, thunder rumbled across the sky and lightning flashed.

Fretting over the delay and his growing

discomfort, Battles peered through the down-pour at the Pullman. All the car's windows were lit up, rectangles of orange in the rain-needled darkness. He thought he heard the chink of glasses from inside and a man's laughter, but because of the dragon hiss of the storm he wasn't sure.

The beautiful officer looked up from the letter he was holding and looked at Battles.

"Come inside, Marshal," he said. He motioned to the soldiers. "One of you take the marshal's horse and see if you can find a place for it out of the rain."

Battles swung out of the saddle and followed the colonel into the Pullman.

He found himself in a small office with a couple of desks. A sergeant orderly sat at one of the desks and rose to his feet when Sinclair and Battles entered.

"Take the marshal's coat and hat, Sergeant," the colonel said. He managed a smile that was neither friendly nor amused. "And try not to drip all over the damned rug."

After Battles shrugged out of his slicker, Sinclair stretched out a hand.

"Please, Marshal, you won't need the firearm," he said.

It was useless to argue the point, and Battles surrendered the Colt.

"It will be here for you when you leave, I

assure you," the colonel said, placing the revolver in his desk drawer.

Sinclair had very white teeth, the canines large, wet, and aggressive, and the marshal pegged him as an ambitious career soldier who had fought all his battles in Washington.

"Wait here," he said.

Sinclair opened the door that led from the office into the main interior of the car and closed it quietly behind him.

The sergeant, a grizzled man with a deeply lined face, had regained his seat behind his desk. He smiled at Battles.

"The colonel can be brusque," he said.

"Some men are," Battles said.

"Officers mostly, the brusque ones."

After a few moments of silence, the soldier said: "You've been through it, Marshal."

"Some."

"You've got the scars. Inside, where they don't show." He smiled again. "But I can see them plain."

Battles studied the man, his hard eyes measuring him. "I could say the same thing about you."

"You could."

The sergeant lapsed into silence again, and then said: "Know what I think?"

Battles said nothing.

"Too many dead men in our pasts, friends and

foe alike. All that dying weighs on a man after a spell."

The marshal's smile again held that amazing warmth and youthfulness. "You're a philosopher, Sergeant."

The old soldier nodded. "Uh-huh, nowadays it's about all that's left to me."

The door opened and Colonel Sinclair entered and looked at Battles.

"The president of the United States will see you now," he said.

Chapter 2

Sinister Forces

President Chester A. Arthur, a waxy-faced man who sported bushy sideburns and a magnificent mustache, sat behind a vast mahogany desk. To his left a thin, long-fingered clerk held a sheaf of papers and affected a worried look. Colonel Sinclair stood behind the president.

Arthur waved Battles into the chair that fronted his desk. He studied the lawman for a few long moments, then said: "Are ye sharp set?"

Battles shook his head. "No, Mr. President, I ate earlier."

"Then a glass of brandy with you?"

"Please," Battles said.

The clerk put his papers on the desk and

12

crossed to a campaign table that held several decanters and a collection of glasses.

He poured brandy for Battles and passed him the drink.

Battles looked at Arthur over the rim of his glass. The president was a sick man that spring of 1882, already suffering from the kidney disease that would kill him five years later, and it showed on him.

"The brandy is to your liking, Marshal?" he said.

Battles nodded. "It's excellent, sir."

"Good, good, very good." Arthur hesitated, then said: "I read your letter of introduction from Governor Roberts. He thinks very highly of you."

Battles smiled. "Then my thanks to the governor."

"Roberts is a good man, but a loyal Democrat," Arthur said. He waved a hand. "It is his one big failing, I'm afraid. Such a pity."

The marshal, wary of politics and politicians, nodded, but said nothing.

"Did Roberts tell you why you're here?" Arthur said, after another pause.

"All he told me was that it has something to do with the letter and map I found on Green River Tom Riley."

Sinclair looked alarmed. "Where is this Riley person now?"

13

"Nowhere. He's dead."

"You killed him?"

"He was notified," Battles said.

"We want no loose ends, Marshal," Sinclair said.

Arthur flashed irritation. "Yes, yes, Colonel. I'll make that clear to Marshal Battles later."

The president leaned forward on his desk.

"We remember President Garfield, Marshal, do we not?" Arthur said.

"Your predecessor, yes, sir."

"Shot by a damned anarchist." Arthur shook his head. "Garfield, that poor, doomed bastard, it took him almost three months to die and him in agony most of the time."

Arthur turned to the clerk and, his voice slightly unsteady, said: "James, brandy. And refill the marshal's glass.

"There were sinister forces at work in this country the day Garfield was assassinated," Arthur said, "and I fear they are still in operation today."

The president downed his brandy and immediately demanded another.

"Look around you, Marshal," Arthur said. "What do you see? An ordinary Pullman railroad car? Let me assure you it is not."

He turned to Sinclair. "Tell him, Colonel."

"The Pullman has two emergency escape hatches," the officer said, "one in the ceiling of the observation lounge, the other in the presidential bedroom at the center of the car."

The colonel tapped on the window beside Arthur's desk. "Three inches of bullet-resistant glass, made by laminating twelve sheets of quarter-inch glass into one piece." He pointed to the walls and ceiling.

"Nickel-steel armor plate, its method of manufacture still a secret, is riveted to the sides, floor, roof, and ends of the car, and the armor is undetectable from any distance."

Sinclair smiled, as though he relished imparting a final secret.

"The weight of a normal Pullman car is eighty tons. This car weighs almost twice that much and can withstand a cannonade."

"And the reason for all this security is that I believe there is a conspiracy afoot to assassinate me and overthrow the legally elected government of this great nation," Arthur said.

Thunder crashed overhead, muted by the thick windows and armor plate of the Pullman. Lightning glimmered, staining parts of the car with sudden flashes of stark white light.

Suddenly Matt Battles figured it out, the reason for him being there. Now he said as much to the president.

"You want me assigned as your bodyguard," he said.

Arthur shook his head. "No such thing, Marshal. You saw the guards outside, and there's a company of the Tenth Cavalry bivouacked within train whistle distance. No, I need greater things from you."

Rather than ask the obvious question, Battles waited.

The car was hot, warmed by a potbellied stove, and the air had grown thick and hard to breathe.

Even the beautiful soldier had tiny beads of sweat on his forehead and nose, but Arthur seemed oblivious.

He turned to the clerk. "My list, James, if you please."

The man dropped a paper in front of Arthur and the president picked it up with both hands.

"I'm going to read you a list of names, Marshal," he said. "I want your comment on each."

"Who are they?" Battles said.

"Gunmen," Colonel Sinclair said, answering for his boss. "Killers, outlaws, men of bad reputation. They hold that in common, but there is one trait more."

The soldier waited until he saw a question form on Battles's face, then said: "There's a score of names on the president's list and every man jack of them has disappeared off the face of the earth over the past month."

Battles smiled. "They're in a dangerous profession, Colonel."

16

"I agree. But for them all to vanish at the same time is just too much of a coincidence, don't you think?"

Arthur spoke again. "I fear these men could have been hired by a person or persons unknown to take part in a desperate venture—perhaps even start a second civil war."

Chapter 3

An Army of Gunmen

It took Matt Battles a few seconds to comprehend what the president was telling him. Then he said: "Sir, the men on your list could be second-raters, wannabes who were trying to make a reputation and ended up with their beards in the sawdust of cow town saloons." He smiled. "It happened to a bunch of them all at once, is all."

"That man you killed down El Paso way, Marshal," Arthur said. "Was he a second-rater, a wannabe, as you say?"

Battles's eyes hardened as he tried to figure whether his honor was in doubt.

Arthur, with a politician's perception, saw the lawman's face stiffen and smiled. "Just an honest question, Marshal. Establishing the man's bona fides, you understand."

Battles took a breath and said: "Like I said

17

earlier, his name was Tom Riley, though sometimes he went by Bob Rawlins. He was a bank and stage robber mostly, but he dabbled in cattle rustling and once did a two-year stint as a city policeman in Denver."

"He was fast with a gun?"

"He was. Riley was real quick and smooth on the draw and shoot."

"And he had a reputation? As a gunman, I mean."

Battles nodded. "He'd killed his share. Riley was a named man."

"A named man? Then he was not a . . . second-rater?"

"He was one of the fastest around. He didn't want to go back to Yuma, was all."

"And you killed him?"

"He'd been notified, but he went for the iron."

"You found a letter on him, Marshal," Arthur said. "And a map."

"Yes." Battles reached into his coat. "I have them here."

Arthur waved a hand. "Later."

He picked up the paper on his desk and settled his pince-nez higher on the bridge of his nose. "Your reaction to these names, Marshal, if you please."

The president cleared his throat, and talked over a sudden burst of thunder. "Joe Dawson."

"Hired gun. Works out of Fannin County, Texas, and gets top dollar. He killed Ed Seagal up in the Nations a while back, and nobody, including me, considered Ed a bargain."

"Dee O'Day."

"Hired killer. Boasts he'll cut any man, woman, or child in half with a shotgun for fifty dollars. And he has."

"Sam Thorne."

"Another hired gun. He's fast and notches his Colts. Last I heard he'd killed seven men, and he's probably added to that total since then."

"Luke Anderson."

"Robber and killer. Likes doves and is suspected of beating one to death with a hammer in Fort Worth."

"The Holbrook Kid."

"Fast gun, operates out of Tucson. Killed a sheriff's deputy in Utah a spell back."

"Chess Thomas."

"Black man. Hired killer. Favors a rifle, even for close work."

"Ben Lane."

"A top-rated Texas gunman and range detective. Once killed a man for calling him Benny, a name he hates. He'll rid your range of rustlers all right, but his services come dear, thirty dollars a day plus expenses."

Arthur stifled a yawn. "I know this grows tedious, Marshal, so one more name at random."

The president's eyes dropped to the bottom of his list. "Juan Duran."

"Goes by the name of Durango. He's a Mexican and Apache breed and they don't come any meaner. He's poison fast with the Colt and usually works the Indian Territory. Ramrods his own gang of murderers, thieves, and rapists, but he's killed more than his share on his own account."

Arthur removed his glasses and pinched the bridge of his nose. When he looked at Battles again, he seemed tired. "Are any of the men I mentioned wannabes or third-raters?"

The marshal smiled and shook his head. "No, sir, you've got the best of the worst."

"All expert gunmen?"

"Every man jack of them."

"And I've got another, what?" His eyes dropped to the list. "Fourteen just like them."

Battles saw the light. "If the rest are as dangerous as the ones you mentioned, then they're an army."

"Exactly. An army of gunmen who all disappeared off the face of the earth at the same time. Why, in God's name, why?"

That last wasn't a question, it was a statement, and Battles said nothing.

Colonel Sinclair stood in front of Battles. He seemed to be wilting a little in the heat of the car.

"May we see the letter now, Marshal, and the map?"

Battles handed the papers over to the soldier, who then turned to Arthur.

"Shall I read the letter aloud to you, sir?"

Arthur nodded.

"Dear Mr. Riley," Sinclair read, "your fame as a daring and desperate outlaw has spread far and wide and I have become your most devoted admirer.

"Thus, I request your most honorable presence at my home at your earliest convenience. Rest assured, if you accept my invitation you will become rich beyond your wildest dreams.

"Enclosed is a map that will guide you to my estate.

"Until we meet, I remain, your obedient servant . . ."

Sinclair laid the letter on Arthur's desk.

"It's signed Hatfield J. Warful," the colonel said.

The president let the letter lie and looked at Battles. "Ever hear of this bird, Marshal?"

Battles shook his head. "No, it's a new one on me."

"Where does the map lead, Colonel?" Arthur said. "North of where we are at present, I take it."

"Yes, north. It would seem to be a place called Slaughter Canyon, Mr. President."

"That's up in the Guadalupe Ridge country," Battles said. "It looks like Warful's location is a mile west of Double Canyon Draw."

"You know that area, Marshal?" Sinclair said.

"Yes, I've been up that way. It's mostly forested country with a backbone of dry mountains that rise seven thousand feet above the trees. The peaks themselves are surrounded by forested flats that stretch to the horizon in all directions."

Battles shook his head. "It's a lost, lonely place that few white men ever visit." He looked at the president. "Who the hell would want to live there?"

"Mr. Warful, evidently," Arthur said. "And what better place to hide a small army of gunmen?"

Chapter 4

Lost Souls

Battles moved in his chair, feeling sweat gather in the small of his back. Despite the car's armor plate, he heard the steam-kettle hiss of the rain and a soldier's rattling cough.

Hardly aware of the clerk refilling his brandy glass, he said: "Mr. President, if all the men on your list got the same letter and map, that means they're bunched up in Slaughter Canyon. Why not send in the Tenth Cavalry to rout them out and arrest Warful?"

Arthur threw up his hands in horror, and Battles was sure he saw his sideburns bristle.

"Marshal, I plan to seek reelection in 'eighty-four and I can't supply ammunition to the damned Democrats. They're already after my hide because I signed the Chinese Exclusion Act, so imagine what they'll do if I use the army to crush a lawful assembly of voting citizens. If blood was spilled—and it would be spilled—they'd crucify me. . . . Why, they'd . . ."

Arthur looked desperately at Sinclair. "Tell him, Colonel, for God's sake."

Sinclair smiled. "Marshal, if we deploy the Tenth and some of those gunmen die, what is to stop Warful from claiming that they were lost souls under his spiritual care?"

"You mean he'd say his place in the mountains was a peaceful retreat for penitent outlaws who deeply regretted their misdeeds?" Battles said.

"Exactly. A peaceful retreat, that is, until the president's bloodthirsty cavalry charged the holy place and cut down the repentant brethren, all good Democrats, with sabers."

Sinclair's smile was wintry. "Imagine what the Democratic press could do with the Massacre at Slaughter Canyon?" He shuddered. "And that's only one scenario. There are others. And remember, women and children could be present. Who knows?"

Battles saw logic in the colonel's fears.

The public would find repenting rogues easier to believe than the premise that the West's top gunmen had pushed aside their differences and had gathered in one place at one time to plot mischief.

The marshal drank his brandy, was wishful of a cigarette, but recalled hearing that the sickly president was down on smoking.

"All right," he said, suddenly tired and increasingly irritable from tobacco hunger. "Where do I come in?"

Sinclair looked at the president. "Shall I sum up, sir?"

Arthur nodded wearily, his skin an odd yellow color.

"Marshal Battles, you will go to Slaughter Canyon, infiltrate the group, and find out what the hell is going on up there," the colonel said.

Battles laughed out loud. "Colonel, half the men on your list know me by sight. And Durango certainly does. I put lead into him three years ago up on the Picketwire and he's held it against me ever since."

"We've taken care of that, Marshal," Sinclair said. "As of now, you're a wanted man yourself."

Before Battles had a chance to speak, Arthur took a gold watch from his vest pocket, thumbed it open, and glanced at the time, the action of a man in a hurry.

"Marshal," he said, "three days ago you robbed the Cattlemen's and Mercantile Bank in Pecos Station, Texas, and killed a teller—"

"A poor Swede boy," Sinclair said.

"And then you rode north along the west bank of the Pecos River, pursued by a posse." Arthur snapped his watch shut. "After one of the pursuing posse members was killed and two wounded, they lost you near the Yeso Hills summit."

Battles's chin dropped to somewhere around his belly button. He tried to talk, but uttered only a dry, strangled croak.

Arthur smiled. "Don't fret, Marshal, we know you didn't rob the bank. The whole thing was set up by the Secret Service on my orders."

"The poor Swede boy you shot was actually an out-of-work actor," Sinclair said. "He was later spirited away to Washington, where he'll remain until this Slaughter Canyon thing is settled. As for the posse you shot up, it never existed."

The colonel passed a newspaper clipping to Battles. "Here, read about it."

Still in shock, Battles scanned the story's cascading headlines.

U.S. DEPUTY MARSHAL TURNS ROGUE

Teller Killed In Bloody Bank Robbery
Poor Swede Boy Hurled Into Eternity In An
Instant By Marshal's Murderous Revolver
Left Weltering In Gore
Grieving Widow Weeps For Loving Spouse
Who Will Ne'er Come Home Again
Rangers Vow To Apprehend Killer

Battles tossed the clip on Arthur's desk.

"You read the account that quickly, Marshal?" he said.

"I've seen enough."

"The story has already appeared in newspapers all over Texas and the New Mexico Territory," the president said. "You've become quite famous."

"And be assured your newfound fame will have already reached the ears of Hatfield J. Warful and his cohorts," Sinclair said. "Now I hope they will readily accept you into their group."

"Maybe," Battles said. "Durango ain't a forgiving man."

"Then you'll have to deal with him, won't you?" the colonel said, his face cold.

Battles made no answer. He no longer cared about Arthur's attitude toward tobacco.

He needed a smoke.

Chapter 5

"Mr. President, This Is Blackmail."

"Please give the marshal another brandy," President Arthur told his clerk. "Poor man looks as though he needs it."

Battles took out the makings, built a smoke, and lit it. He let the clerk refill his glass.

"Tobacco is a friend to many," Arthur said, frowning. "But it's a devil in disguise."

The marshal let that go and said: "Mr. President, you set all this up days ago, while I was still on the trail from Texas?"

Arthur smiled. "My dear Marshal Battles, we set it up, as you say, weeks ago, after we learned about the strange disappearance of the gunfighters."

Battles dragged smoke deep into his lungs and felt the tobacco work its relaxing magic. "Why me?"

"Because you were the best man for the job." The president turned to Sinclair. "Is that not so, Colonel?"

"Indeed, sir," the soldier said. He looked at Battles. "You came highly recommended, Marshal, a man of integrity, courage, and skill at arms. But more important, you have intelligence enough to pass yourself off as a rogue lawman on the scout."

"And if I say no?" Battles asked.

"Then you will turn in your star right now," the president said. "After that, as Mr. Battles, you will have to take your chances on the robbery and murder charges."

"Trumped-up charges," Battles said.

"I'm sure the Secret Service can find ways to make them stick," Arthur said.

Battles was stung. "Mr. President, this is blackmail."

Arthur smiled without humor. "You choose an ugly word, Marshal. Let's just call it persuasion."

"Well, will you do it?" Sinclair asked. His eyes were hard, like green ice. "Your country needs you at this critical time."

"Do I have a choice?"

"I'm afraid not."

Battles felt defeat weigh on him. "Then I guess I've got to do it."

Arthur and Colonel Sinclair looked visibly relieved.

"Crackerjack!" the president said. "As I said earlier you will infiltrate the group, learn what you can about Warful and his plans, and report back here, to this place."

"I'll tent here for two weeks with a company of the Tenth, Marshal," Sinclair said. "If, after that time, I haven't heard from you, I'll assume you're dead and make alternative plans accordingly."

Battles's smile was bleak. "It sounds like I'm one expendable lawman."

"Well, that goes with the badge you wear, does it not?" Sinclair said.

Arthur rose to his feet.

"The hour grows late and I'm sure you're eager to be on your way," he said. "My clerk will see that you're provisioned from my own supplies."

He stuck out his hand. "Well, good luck, Marshal Battles."

When Battles took his proffered hand, the president said: "When this enterprise is successfully concluded, there could be advancement in it for you. Is that not so, Colonel?"

"Indeed," Sinclair said, with a notable lack of enthusiasm, as though the petty promise of promotion to a civilian was beneath the notice of a soldier.

He looked at Battles, dismissing him with his glance. "Two weeks, Marshal. Make them count."

Matt Battles reckoned that the president didn't live very high on the hog, judging by the supplies his clerk stuffed in a burlap sack.

"I've packed enough for a couple of days, Marshal," he said. "That's all the colonel said you'd need. Salt pork, hardtack and half a loaf of sourdough bread. Oh, and I included a tin cup and coffee."

He smiled like a conspirator plotting the death of Caesar. "And I tossed in a pint of Old Crow to keep out the night chill."

Battles took the sack. "I'm obliged."

The clerk said, "Well, good luck, Marshal."

"Thanks," Battles said. "Something tells me I'm gonna need it."

Chapter 6

The Quitter

It was still full dark when Matt Battles headed north, allowing his stud to pick its way through the rain-lashed gloom.

He paid little heed to the downpour, a man used to hard times, making do, doing without. He had seldom slept within the sound of church bells, and the parlous confines of his world were bounded by mountains, deserts, and rivers and were populated by sudden and violent men.

Battles had killed seven such men, five in fair fights, two while fleeing arrest. None of the seven haunted his dreams o' nights.

He was a lean six feet, honed down by sun, wind, and winter snows to a whipcord one hundred and seventy pounds. He was as hard as an iron nail and many times more enduring.

Battles was thirty-six that summer, but his eyes were older, faded, as though worn out by things he'd done and seen. Unyielding, dogged, steadfast, staunch, resolute, tough, fearless in the gunfight— he was all of those things and more besides.

Of love and the softening influence of a woman, he knew nothing. He enjoyed the female body and took sexual pleasure where and when he could find it.

He had visited many towns and none therein was glad at his coming or sad at his leaving.

Lonely and dangerous as a lobo wolf, Matt Battles was named by some as the most effective U.S. Marshal to ever wear a star. He was unaware of that description and if he had known, he would've taken no pride in it.

The rain fell steadily. The thunderstorm was now a ways off, but it circled in the distance, growling, flashing, waiting its chance to pounce again.

Battles reckoned the New Mexico border was three miles ahead of him. Soon he'd pick up the dark bulk of the Guadalupe Ridge.

Around him stretched a rocky land forested by wild oak, piñon, and juniper, here and there, shimmering silver in the lighting flare, meadows of grass where wildflowers bloomed.

Trusting to the buckskin's instincts and his own far-seeing eyes, Battles swung east around the deep chasm of Gunsight Canyon, then splashed across the Black River, low at this time of the year, months after the spring melt.

He fetched onto the opposite bank, then fought his startled horse for a few moments as the big stud attempted to turn and run.

What the hell?

Then Battles saw what the horse had seen.

A young man's body swung from the crooked limb of a cottonwood, the toes of the boots he wore dangling just a few inches off the ground. His neck was straight, the hemp rope just under his chin.

"They could've been white men enough to have at least broke your neck, couldn't they, son?" Battles said.

He swung out of the saddle and let the uneasy buckskin sidestep away a few yards.

Rain rattling around him, Battles studied the dead man's distorted features.

He didn't know him.

He was a good-looking towheaded kid, the kind of boy girls love to take home to Mother. The crossed gun belts around his narrow hips—the revolvers gone—marked him as a wannabe. Only a tyro wore a gun rig like that.

The marshal ripped the cardboard placard from around the boy's neck. The rain had softened the paper, but the lettering, in red paint, was still readable. QUITTER.

"What did you quit, boy?" Battles said. "Or who?"

The dead kid's half-opened eyes stared at him in the flashing darkness, seeing nothing, revealing nothing.

Battles reached under his slicker, found his Barlow knife, and cut the boy down, catching his body before it thumped to the ground.

In the marshal's world, even the hurting dead were due at least a small measure of respect.

The marshal laid the kid on his back and noticed something white sticking out of his shirt pocket. The rain shredded the wet paper in Battles's fingers, but he recognized it for what it was—a letter similar to the one he'd taken from Tom Riley's body.

Hatfield J. Warful had also sent this kid an invitation.

He looked at the young face more closely, wiping away rainwater accumulated in the boy's eye sockets.

He shook his head.

No, he'd never seen the kid before.

Some time back he'd read a reward dodger for a youngster wanted in connection with a stagecoach robbery and murder.

This could be him.

Or he could be any number of other reckless young men who longed to be a badman of reputation like that Lincoln County hellion Billy the Kid.

Although the night was far gone, Battles had enough of riding through rain and he was wishful for coffee, if such could be made in a frog strangler.

But no shelter was to be found, and there was no dry wood, not even a twig. He settled for a seat under the cottonwood, fetching his back against the trunk as the returning thunderstorm raved around him and lightning shattered the sky.

The omen arrived ten minutes later, as Battles smoked his second sodden cigarette amid raindrops that ticked through the foliage of the tree.

Does fate, destiny, call it what you will, now and then send a man a herald to warn him that his present course is doomed to disaster?

Matt Battles, a simple man living in a simpler time, believed that it did.

The lightning bolt was accompanied by a bang that sounded as though the top had blown off a mountain.

Branches crashed around Battles as the trunk split and for a brief moment flames fluttered above him like scarlet moths.

Panicked, he yelped, rolled away from the now V-shaped trunk. He didn't stop rolling until he was a dozen yards away. Then he sat up, his eyes big as coins.

After a few moments Battles rose groggily to his feet. Lightning scrawled across the sky like a signature on his death warrant, and the rain-riven night smelled of sulfur and fire.

The marshal tipped back his head and vented his lungs. After his string of cussing ran out, he shouted: "Well, damn it, Lord, I know we ain't exactly on speakin' terms, but did you have to try and kill me?"

Thunder roared an angry answer, and with that, the realization came to Matt Battles that God hadn't really taken a pot at him—the lightning strike had been a sign, a warning that he should get the hell out of the New Mexico Territory.

The last scarlet moth died in the shattered cottonwood as Battles summed things up in his mind and made his decision.

He was acting like the old maid who hears a rustle in every bush. Omen or no omen, he was here to carry out the president's orders.

There was only him, nobody else.

He had it to do.

Chapter 7

Cold-blooded Murder

It's a hard thing to leave a man unburied, but Matt Battles had no choice.

However, he did what he could. He straightened the boy's body, crossed his arms, and wished him well on his journey.

The thunderstorm had fled in a sulk an hour before sunrise, throwing black clouds around it like a cloak before stomping south.

Now Battles rode into the dawning day as the yellow haze of the aborning sun filtered through the water-ticking foliage of the junipers and wild oaks.

After an hour, the terrain changed, abruptly becoming more typical of the northern reaches of the Chihuahuan Desert, a sandy wasteland of brush, catclaw, sotol, cholla, and most of their thorny relatives.

Battles drew rein, a solitary horseman in a vast wilderness of mountain and sky that reduced him into a speck of insignificance.

He built a cigarette and thought about Hatfield Warful.

Why would anyone make his home in this godforsaken place?

Warful obviously wanted to hide from the world, which raised another question—why?

The obvious answer was so he could secretly recruit the twenty fastest gunmen in the West for some crackpot scheme of his.

Battles drew deep on his cigarette, trying to puzzle it through.

But again, why here?

There were plenty of greener and more pleasant pastures in the western lands where outlaws could hide out. Just ask the James boys.

No, there had to be some other reason for Warful choosing Slaughter Canyon, but Battles was damned if he could figure what it might be.

Well, studying on it was getting him nowhere and neither was sitting his horse. He stubbed out his cigarette butt on a boot heel and kneed the buckskin forward.

Time would answer all of his questions, he was sure.

If he lived that long.

The craggy rock walls of Slaughter Canyon rose sheer from the flat, its towering peaks and bluffs so dark in color as to be almost black.

A few stunted junipers struggled on the steep slopes, battling yucca and barbed entanglements of prickly pear for living space.

The climbing sun hammered the canyon with glaring white heat, and there was no wind. Battles's shirt darkened with sweat, and under his hatband his forehead itched.

He saw the three riders when they were still a ways off, men and horses elongated in a shimmering haze.

Battles drew rein and adjusted the Colt in his waistband. The corners of his eyes crinkled as he scanned the distance, trying to make out the mood and manner of the oncoming horsemen.

The president had told him that news of the

bank robbery and murder would've preceded him. He hoped so. A gunfight with three men within the barren confines of the canyon was not a prospect he relished.

His worst fears were confirmed as the riders regained their normal shape and size and spread out slightly as they came closer.

Battles recognized Durango, his wide sombrero marking him as the breed gunman. Flanking Durango to his right was Charlie, a black killer with a beautiful baritone voice. Judging by the scowl on Charlie's face, he planned to sing a different tune that morning.

The third rider, a loose-geared man with yellow hair falling over his shoulders, was Dee O'Day, and he was about as mean as they came.

Battles sat his saddle, smiling, seemingly relaxed. But inside, his stomach had tied itself in a knot.

When the riders were within hailing distance, Battles's smile grew into a grin and he said: "Howdy, boys. Hot today, ain't it?"

Durango drew rein and the others did the same.

"Good to see you again, Matt," the breed said. "I've been looking forward to it."

It was not a friendly greeting; it was a threat, and Battles recognized it as such, but he pretended otherwise. "You too, Durango. I trust you're in good health."

"All right for a man who's still carrying the lead you put into him."

Battles's concern was as genuine as Durango's greeting had been.

"Your right thigh, wasn't it?" he said.

"Left."

Battles nodded. "I'm real sorry about the leg. I was shooting a new Winchester that morning and she was holding a tad low."

"I'll kill you one day, Matt," Durango said, his words flat, emotionless, like lead slugs dropping into a tin coin box.

Battles nodded. "I reckon you'll try, Durango. You know where to find me."

Charlie looked at Battles with hard black eyes.

"Heard about the bank you robbed, and the killing," he said. "Says you gunned a poor Swede boy."

"News travels fast," Battles said.

"Lem Wilson rode in day afore yesterday, brung a newspaper," Charlie said. "The story and your mug was on the front page."

"The paper says you stole ten thousand in gold," Durango said.

"The story says right."

"Then where's the money?"

Battles thought fast. "Hid it," he said. "In a limestone cave down in the Sierra Diablo country."

Durango stared at him. He was a swarthy man in his late twenties with lank black hair and a great beak of a nose overhanging a thin pencil mustache. His eyes were a startling green, inherited from the Irish laborer father he never knew, a striking contrast to the Mexican bandito costume and wide sombrero he affected.

"I don't believe you hid it," he said finally. "I think you being here is a setup and there never was any money, or any killing either."

"You saying I'm a liar, Durango?" Battles said.

The man nodded. "Yeah, I'm calling it."

Battles had run out of room on the dance floor. The last thing he wanted was a gunfight, but to let Durango's insult go would've marked him as a coward and a man not to be trusted. He'd blow any chance he ever had of penetrating Warful's group.

Besides, he wasn't near sure he could shade Durango.

Charlie saved him.

"Durango, I believe what I read in the newspapers," Charlie said. "I say we let the boss decide if this is a setup or no."

He looked at Battles, studying him.

"Matt Battles, I've always knowed you fer an upright lawman," he said. "And I tell you this: If you're lying to us and this whole thing is a lawman's trickery, you'll die hard. Afore it's over, you'll curse the day you were born and the mother that bore you."

Charlie leaned forward in the saddle. "Is my meanin' clear?"

"As day," Battles said.

Durango wouldn't let it go, at least not yet.

"Still drawing from the waistband, huh, Matt?" he said.

"As good a way as any."

"Maybe. For a damned sodbuster."

Battles swallowed the barb and mentally took a step back. He couldn't allow Durango to push him into a fight.

"Back off, Durango," Charlie said. "I told you to let the boss handle this."

The breed nodded, smiling. His teeth were small and white.

"You can't shade me, Matt," he said. "Not now, not ever."

Durango moved, the fast strike of a rattlesnake.

Suddenly a Colt sprang into his hand and he fired.

Stunned, Charlie looked down at the blood blossoming in the center of his chest. But only for a moment. He stood in the stirrups, said something deep in his throat, and toppled from the saddle.

"I don't take orders from your kind," Durango said.

A man long used to violence, Battles was still shocked by the suddenness of the killing. He had witnessed the cold-blooded murder of an

unprepared man, a spur-of-the-moment dem-
onstration of his prowess by an expert gunman
who valued life cheaply.

Durango glanced at Battles, then at Dee O'Day.

"You heard Charlie," he said. "Let's go talk to
the boss."

Chapter 8

A Great Enterprise

Durango led the way to an arroyo that doglegged
to the north off the main canyon. The heat,
trapped by bare rock walls, was stifling and the
air smelled of dust.

Battles's curiosity got the better of him and he
said to Durango: "Are we close to Warful's
estate?"

The gunman grinned. "What estate? He lives in
a damned tent."

Durango gave the marshal a sidelong glance.
"He's got a woman with him."

"I'd guess beautiful, huh?"

"Yeah, if you like a gal that dresses out at
around four hundred pounds."

Durango bit on a black cheroot, then thumbed
a match into flame. Speaking around the lighted
cigar, he said: "She stinks like she's got a goat
under each arm and a dead fish between her
legs."

"Durango, you're telling me way too much that I don't want to know," Battles said.

The breed grinned. "You'll find out."

Imagine a man standing seven feet tall, weighing less than a hundred and fifty pounds. Now, dress him in a suit that looks like an undertaker's castoff. Add a completely bald head, a face like a skull, the skin tight to the bones, and eyes the color of bleach.

Sum it all up in your mind and you have a picture of Hatfield J. Warful.

The man stood outside his tent, flanked by a couple of gunmen, and watched as Durango rode closer, leading Charlie's horse.

Durango tossed the reins to O'Day and swung out of the saddle.

He walked up to Warfield, then did something that surprised the hell out of Battles. Durango slammed his clenched fist into the middle of his chest and gave a little bow from the waist.

Warful mirrored the gesture and smiled, a horse-toothed grimace that held more menace than humor.

Durango, his flared black pants cut skintight to his butt, leaned closer to Warful and started to talk urgently, gesturing to Battles and beyond him to the canyon.

After he was done, Warful merely nodded and clapped a hand on Durango's shoulder in a

43

gesture of dismissal. He waited until the breed had drawn off a ways before he beckoned Battles closer.

The marshal figured his concocted story was about to meet its biggest test, and the thought stirred no joy in him. Warful looked like a man who would take a heap of convincing.

Battles stepped out of the leather and walked toward the giant, his hand extended and what he hoped was a friendly grin on his face.

"Matt Battles," he said, "and I'm right glad to meet you, Mr. Warful."

Warful ignored Battles's hand, and instead made that clenched fist gesture again. Feeling like a fool, the marshal did the same.

"Your fame precedes you, Marshal Battles. Or should I say Mr. Battles?"

"Mister sets just fine by me," Battles said.

"I read of your exploits when you were still a lawman, of course," Warful said, "and I must confess to a certain disappointment."

The giant smiled. "I would have expected you to be at least ten feet tall and of heroic countenance, but now I see you are really quite ordinary."

Battles decided to keep his mouth shut. The least said the better.

Besides, what the hell did "of heroic countenance" mean?

A silence fell between the two men and Warful let it stretch so long that Battles began to feel uncomfortable.

Finally the gaunt giant said: "Why are you here?"

Now Battles decided he was on firmer ground.

"I heard you were hiring gun hands," he said.

"And how did you know this?"

The marshal, a crick in his neck from trying to look into Warful's eyes as a mark of sincerity, said: "I took a letter off a dead man that you'd mailed to him."

"What was his name?"

"The day he died, he was going by Tom Riley."

"And you killed him?"

"He gave me no choice."

"In the line of duty?"

"Yeah, I was still a marshal at the time."

Battles decided now was the time to spin the big windy. "After I read your letter, well, that's when I decided to rob the Pecos City Bank and head directly for Slaughter Canyon," he said, blinking.

Warful nodded. "Not directly, it seems. Durango tells me you took time to hide ten thousand dollars in a cave."

"He told you right."

"There's a cave right here in the canyon. You could have hidden it there."

"I didn't know that."

"Pah," Warful said, spreading his hands, "we stand here talking about pennies when millions are at stake."

"What do you have in mind?" Battles said, knowing he was pushing it.

The giant looked down at him from his great height. "When the time is right, I'll tell you. Let me just say that a great enterprise is unfolding and I may allow you to become part of it."

He beckoned to Durango. "Take the marshal's gun."

It had been only a four-word speech, but it contained two implied threats Battles didn't like. The first was obvious; the second was the use of the word "marshal."

Did that last mean that Warful was wary of trusting him?

Grinning, Durango held out a hand. "The iron . . . Marshal."

Warful noted Battles's growing irritation and smiled. "Don't be alarmed, Mr. Battles. It's only a temporary measure." This time he laid emphasis on the "mister." He laid a hand on Battles's shoulder. "Soon, once I get to know you better, we will become perfect friends and your revolver will be returned to you."

But Matt Battles was a stubborn man and could only be prodded so far and no further.

He worked it out in his mind.

Durango first because he was the fastest with

the iron. Then Warful. And the whole damned thing would be over with. He'd be killed himself, of that he had no doubt. The men flanking their boss would see to it. But better that than die of shame by surrendering his gun to a lowlife like Durango.

Battles took a step back and turned slightly so he had Durango in his line of vision.

"I'm not giving my gun to that piece of dung," he said to Warful. "Or to any like him."

Chapter 9

Blacks and Jews

Durango was mad clean through. His killing rage made him look like a man possessed. His right hand was clawed above the handle of his gun.

"I'll take the iron off your damned corpse," he said.

"Enough!" Warful said.

He glared at Durango. "If Mr. Battles wishes to keep his sidearm, then let him. Keep a closer eye on him, though. Until he proves his loyalty."

"I hung one just like you, Matt," Durango said. "A damned turncoat who planned to sell us out."

"I saw him, Durango," Battles said, his own anger rising. "He was just a boy. About your style, I reckon."

"Durango, let it go," Warful said. "Go get

yourself a drink and a cigar at the commissary and calm down." He tensed, and the gunmen flanking him did the same. "That's an order, mister."

Durango's face stiffened as he fought a battle with himself. Then, breathing noisily through his beak of a nose, he visibly relaxed.

Finally he said, his eyes blazing, "This is over for now, Matt. You won't be so lucky the next time."

He spun on his heel and strode away.

Warful smiled. "Durango is emotional and highly strung. The greaser half of him is to blame, I fear."

"He really did hang the boy?" Battles said.

"On my orders, yes. Does it trouble you?"

"I don't like seeing any man hung."

"The boy knew too much, that we are gathered here for a great and noble venture. I could not let him leave and risk him reporting us to the authorities."

A silence stretched between the two men; then Warful said: "How did you feel about Durango gunning Charlie, Mr. Battles?"

"It was cold-blooded murder."

"Perhaps so, but Charlie should've remembered to keep a civil tongue in his head around white men."

"Durango is only half white," Battles said. "He's a breed."

He couldn't believe he'd just said that. It was as though all his dormant prejudices had suddenly bubbled to the surface of his conscience.

"Yes, yes, he is," Warful said. "And that is a state of affairs I will address at a later date."

Before Battles could respond, Warful said: "How do you feel about blacks and Jews in general, the subhuman races?"

Battles shrugged and treaded warily. "I never really thought about them much."

"Do you know any Jews?"

"Only one, I guess, Sam Glattstein, owns a saloon and poolroom down Austin way."

"What do you think of him?"

"Sam? Well, his beer is cold and he pours an honest drink. He's also been known to spot a down-on-his-luck cowboy a beer and a meal if he's riding the grub line."

"Where you find one Jew, there are many more," Warful said. "Down Austin way, I'm willing to bet there's a major infestation."

"I wouldn't know about that," Battles said.

"Ah, but you will, never fear, because I'll educate you in such matters," Warful said.

Battles now pegged the man and for the first time realized the enormity of what he was facing.

Warful was a crackpot and that made him all the more dangerous.

Did he plan to use his outlaw gunmen to kill

blacks and Jews, people he obviously hated?

If that was the case, Battles was all that stood between those folks and a massacre.

The giant was talking again.

"I grow weary, Mr. Battles." He gestured toward a man at his side. "Mr. Lon Stuart here will show you to your quarters."

Stuart was a tall, loose-limbed man with reptilian eyes and a bullet scar on his left cheek.

"Mr. Stuart will also show you our commissary," Warful said. "It's stocked with the finest liquors and cordials and a range of excellent cigars." He smiled. "Free of charge, of course."

Warful pulled back his tent flap and Battles was hit by a stinking wave that hit him like a fist.

"My lady wife is taking her beauty nap," Warful said. "But you will meet her later."

Battles decided to play the game and said with a straight face. "It will be the pleasure of my day."

Lon Stuart stopped outside a tent in the middle of a row of others. "You'll bunk here with Dee O'Day," he said. He nodded to a larger tent opposite, a couple of wagons parked behind it. "That there's the commissary. Help yourself."

The man turned to walk away, but Battles

said: "Are you the Lon Stuart out of Brewster County?"

The man smiled, his eyes holding all the warmth of a Louisiana swamp alligator.

"Mister," he said, "I'm the Lon Stuart out of hell."

Chapter 10

The Question

"What do you think of him?"

"I can use him."

The enormously obese woman on the oversized cot bit into an expensive Belgian bonbon, then studied its pink center.

Without looking at Warful, she said: "Do you believe him?"

"I haven't yet made up my mind, my dear."

"I don't."

"A leopard can't change its spots, huh?"

"A federal lawman can't."

Warful made a resigned face. "We'll see. I can always dispose of him after the conquest."

"What's his opinion of the Jewish question?"

"He knows a good Jew."

"There are no good Jews."

"I will educate him to that fact, my dear."

The woman popped the bonbon into her scarlet mouth.

"I'm tired of this awful place, Hatfield," she said, chewing. "When can I wear silk again and get rid of this cotton shift?"

"We'll leave soon, Hattie. I assure you."

"When do the wagons leave the Comstock?"

Warful smiled. "You know that as well as I do, dear one. We'll embark on a westbound train in three days."

"And the sailing ship?"

"It will be there."

"Do you trust that captain . . . what's his name?"

"Poke Yates. Yes, I trust him. He's a damned pirate, but his ship will be at the dock. He thinks as we do, my love, and he's just as anxious for plunder as the rest of the scum I have around me."

The woman rooted around in her chocolate box like a great she-bear ransacking a beehive.

"I dread a long train journey, Hatfield," she said without looking up. "It's so very tedious."

Warful reached out and squeezed the vast pillow of his wife's breast.

"Very soon now you'll ride in your own private train," he said. "In a land that is ours."

Hattie smiled. "Hasten the day, my love."

"Indeed," Warful said.

"The Afrikaners will come?"

"I've been assured of a force of five hundred mounted rifles," Warful said. "More than enough for our purposes."

"And the British and French? I don't trust the British."

"The Boers bloodied British noses at Mujaba Hill a couple of months ago and now all their problems lie in the south. They won't interfere. Nor will the French as long as we don't intrude on one of their colonies."

The woman sighed. "Politics, politics. It's all so complicated."

Warful shook his head. "It's really not. You'll see."

Hattie turned in the bed to face Warful. The cloying stench of her body was a palpable thing. "Will the Jews fight?"

"They've never done so before and there have been many pogroms in many nations."

"I want you to get me a Jewish wedding ring, Hatfield."

The man's skull face broke into a grin. "Never fear, Hattie. After this is done I'll have hundreds for you."

Chapter 11

The South Will Rise Again

Dee O'Day was a killer and a talking man.

"Damn, I'll be glad to get away from this place," he said. "I used to think the world was a big place, but it's shrunk to the walls of this canyon."

"You're an open-range man, Dee, huh?" Battles said.

"Yeah, except when I'm on the scout."

O'Day, stripped to his long johns, lay on his back on his cot, a bottle of whiskey balanced on his lean belly.

"You take towns, now," he said. "I like towns if they've got snap."

He turned his head and looked at Battles. "You ever been in Denver?"

"Can't say as I have," Battles said.

"Denver has snap," O'Day said.

"I must ride up there one day," Battles said.

"Nah," O'Day said, "you ain't the kind for Denver. With that long face of your'n you look too much like a preacher. Put folks off their sinnin'." He smiled. "No offense, mind."

"None taken."

The tent was stifling hot and smelled of booze and man sweat.

Outside, the hammering sun made sure that nothing moved in the heat but the insects that droned or chirped in the brush.

Battles sat on the edge of his cot and built a cigarette. He lit the smoke and accepted the bottle proffered by O'Day. He took a swig and passed it back.

"What's Warful up to, Dee?" he said.

The young gunman's head moved on his sodden pillow. "How the hell should I know? He

54

doesn't confide in me. He hasn't even told Durango, and for some reason he sets store by that breed."

O'Day looked at Battles, his face serious. "I'll tell you what I think. I think he plans to take Richmond, then raise the flag of the Confederacy."

"Start another civil war?"

"That's what I think. Whatever Warful has in mind, it's big. Mighty big."

O'Day took a slug from the bottle, wiped his mouth with the back of his hand, then said: "You're a lawman, Battles. What's your opinion?"

"You mean I was a lawman."

"Maybe you are, maybe you ain't. Anyhow, let me hear it. What's Warful's plan?"

"I've no idea. Maybe it's what you said"—he poked a hole in the air with a forefinger—"the South will rise again."

O'Day grinned. "Sure way to get all our heads blowed off. The damned Yankees killed my daddy and my three older brothers at Gettysburg. Me, I don't want anything to do with any civil war junk."

"He says he'll make us rich, Dee," Battles said. "That much I do know."

"Yeah, and it's the reason why I'm still here. He better tell us soon how he plans to do that or I'm hauling my freight."

"Somebody already tried," Battles said. "Last night I found him hanging from a cottonwood."

"He was him, he wasn't Dee O'Day or a patch on me. Warful knows that if he comes after me with a rope he'll be the first to die and his damned breed of his'n will be the second."

The gunman looked at Battles again. "You seen his wife? Her name's Hattie."

"Smelled her. That was enough."

"Would you do her?"

"Hell no. You?"

"I could never get drunk enough for that," O'Day said.

Battles dropped his cigarette butt and ground it under his heel.

"Yeah, that's right, Marshal," O'Day said. "Mess up the place."

Battles smiled. "What's that salute everybody gives, the clenched-fist thing?"

"It's Warful's idea, says it's a white man's salute that them ancient Romans invented. He's got some pretty strange notions, about Jews an' sich."

"What about Jews?"

"He's agin them. Says . . ." The gunman thought for a few moments to get it right. "Says all the woes of mankind have been caused by Jews, all the wars and plagues an' stuff."

"You know any Jews, Dee?"

"Nary a one. But I'll tell you this much, pay me fifty dollars an' I'll shoot a Jew as quick as I would any other man, or woman come to that."

"You're true blue, Dee," Battles said, making no attempt to disguise the irony of his tone.

"Damn right I am," Dee O'Day said, nodding.

Chapter 12

Two Tons of Gold

Matt Battles kicked his heels around camp for the next couple of days. He explored the canyon, looking for old Indian sign, but found nothing.

The reaction of the gunmen to his presence varied from wary sociability to indifference to downright hostility.

By nature, men who lived by the gun tended to be short on talk and long on watching, O'Day and Durango being notable exceptions. Most had careful eyes that looked at nothing directly but saw everything.

Battles knew well that he was under constant scrutiny, his comings and goings noted, distrust following him like his own shadow.

Bored, he even found himself looking forward to the meals prepared by Mosey, Warful's black cook and water hauler. The food was filling, if monotonous because the menu never varied—bacon and beans for breakfast, steak and beans for dinner. But Mosey's coffee was good and his biscuits, when he was in the mood, sublime.

A drinking man by times, Battles took a bottle from the commissary but drank from it rarely, unlike O'Day, who cheerfully downed a quart of rye a day.

Of Warful he saw little and the lanky giant largely ignored him. He seemed preoccupied, totally absorbed in his thoughts.

Battles had still no hint of the man's plans, though O'Day's suggestion that he aimed to start a second civil war seemed as logical as any.

Then, on the evening of Battles's third day in camp, everything changed.

Warful ordered his men to gather around the commissary tent. He stood on an Arbuckle coffee box and waited until all had gathered before speaking.

"We all know that the Comstock mines pretty much played out a couple of years ago, but our interest is not in silver," he said. He hesitated a moment before adding: "It's gold."

A murmur of appreciation rose from the assembled gunmen. Silver, at two thousand dollars a ton, might make a man rich, but slowly. Gold they understood and appreciated.

"The last gold shipment to leave the Comstock will arrive in San Francisco by train in a week, there to be loaded into the hold of the bark *Lila*, Captain Poke Yates commanding."

"How much gold, boss?"

This from Ben Lane, the Texas fast-draw artist and a questioning man by nature.

"Two tons, packed in small kegs bound with iron hoops," Warful said.

"How much is that worth in American money?" another man said.

"One and a half million dollars, give or take," Warful said.

A few men broke into cheers and Dee O'Day yelled: "Hell, if we split it . . . what? . . . nineteen ways . . . that's . . . that's . . ." His mind grappled with the figures. "A lot."

"It's enough money for a man to live like a king for ten lifetimes," Lane said.

Battles decided to play up his badman role.

"What do we do, boss?" he said. "Rob the train?"

Warful shook his head. The dying sun gleamed on his bald head, and his eyes held a prophet's fire.

"Too risky," he said. "The train will be well guarded and even if we overcame the opposition, we'd need wagons and mules to transport the load. Slowed by wagons like that, we'd be caught before we put a dozen miles between us and the rails."

"Then how do we play it?" Battles said.

"Why, we walk on board the good ship *Lila* as honored guests and put to sea."

Now a murmur of doubt buzzed through the men, and Warful smiled and raised his hands for silence.

"Listen to me," he said. "The entire gold shipment was purchased by an Indian prince and—"

"What tribe?" O'Day said.

"Not a redskin, a prince who lives in the distant land of India," Warful said, his scowling face revealing little patience for O'Day's lack of intelligence.

"Now, this prince—his name escapes me but it doesn't matter—chartered Captain Yates's bark to carry the gold from San Francisco to his home in Bangalore, India." Warful smiled. "That was his big mistake. Oh, Captain Yates will transport the gold all right, but not to India."

O'Day, half drunk, clapped his hands and grinned.

"Now I get it," he said. "We gun the crew, take over the ship, and land the gold somewhere, and nobody the wiser."

O'Day looked around for the approval that he felt his shrewdness merited, but Warful stopped him.

"That is not the plan, Mr. O'Day," he said. "It could be, if you're willing to clutch at thousands, but I can show you a way to make millions." He looked at Ben Lane. "Enough, Mr. Lane, for an 'undred lifetimes."

"What's the play, boss?" Lane said.

"That will be revealed when we're safely aboard ship and out at sea with a fair wind at our backs," Warful said.

Battles asked a question that must have been on a few minds, because several of the gunmen nodded their approval.

"Boss," he said, trying to flatter Warful into candidness, "aren't you taking a lot on trust? How do you know the gold will leave the Comstock on time, and that the ship will even be there?"

"Good questions, Marshal Battles," Warful said. "Thoughtful questions, I'll be bound." His face did not change expression. "Through a shipping agent in San Francisco, the prince chartered Captain Yates's bark a full six months ago, when myself and my lady wife were still residents of that fair city."

He looked around his audience, then talked directly at Battles.

"San Francisco was largely built with Comstock silver," he said, "so shipments into the city usually went unnoticed. But the gold generated a deal of interest because it was said to be the last that would ever leave the mines and had been purchased by an eastern potentate. Its time of arrival at the docks is therefore not a secret."

Warful managed a reassuring smile. "Don't worry, the good ship *Lila* will be there, and so will the gold."

Lane took a step forward. "If you arranged all this with the captain, what do you need us for? We're guns for hire, not sailors."

"I'll tell you what for, Mr. Lane," Warful said. "You men will be aboard the *Lila* to guard against black-hearted treachery. Poke Yates long ago took a set as an honest seaman, but in truth he's a pirate rogue who has sent many a fine craft to the bottom, aye, and their crews with them. Captain Yates is not above slitting a throat or two if it suits his purposes, and that's why his *Lila* carries a crew of twenty-five, twice the normal complement."

Warful waved a hand, taking in the entire crowd. "The captain claims he's an honest seaman. Well, you men are here to make damned sure he stays that way."

Chapter 13

Teetering on a Knife-Edge

Matt Battles considered that so far Warful's speech had been plausible, but the man was holding something back. He had other plans for the gold, and an equal division of the spoils was clearly not one of them.

Then Warful's voice rose to what was almost a scream, and Battles heard the man plumb the depths of his madness.

"Before you men leave," he said, "listen to a tale of treachery that has already happened and that you should all know about. My lady wife and I once had a thriving business in that part of San Francisco they call the Barbary Coast. We rented out young Chinese girls by the hour, day, week, and considered them nonhumans, disposable commodities. But then, when the paying customers murdered too many of the sluts, we were forced out."

Spittle formed at the corners of his mouth. He lifted his head and clutched convulsively at his chest.

"By the Jews!" he shrieked.

Tears welled in Warful's eyes and he tore at his shirt. "The San Francisco police ran me out of town. But who owns the police department? The

Jews! Who controls the finances of the city? The Jews! Who were jealous of my success and wanted my business for their own? The Jews!"

Warful bent his head, and his shoulders heaved and he fell into a sobbing silence.

Battles looked around him and saw a mix of bafflement and disbelief on the faces of the gunmen.

Talk to them of range wars, nesters, train and stage robberies, the business of killing men for a price, and they would listen. But Warful's mad tirade was something beyond their experience and they didn't know what to make of it.

And the man was mad, Battles had no doubt of that. And now he feared that the demons that possessed Warful could drag all of them into a hell of his own making.

Now the man began to talk—no, not talk, scream—again, spittle flying from his lips.

"I will have my revenge on the Jew, and every man jack of you will help me," he said. "We will destroy them with fire and sword wherever they may be found, take what is theirs, and make sport with their wives and daughters."

"Heehaw!" O'Day yelled. "Now you're talkin', boss. For a share of the gold, we'll shoot anybody you want, an' . . . an' do their daughters."

A few men laughed, but most were as perplexed as before and said nothing. Even Durango, a conscienceless killer if ever there was one, seemed doubtful, as though Warful's apparent madness could send this whole crooked enterprise cartwheeling out of control.

But Warful lifted his head and seemed to have regained his composure, studying the men before him with dry eyes.

"Gentlemen," he said, "at first light we leave for Pecos City, where we'll take the train for San Francisco." He paused a moment, then yelled, throwing his arms wide: "And then on to untold riches!"

His words had the desired effect. Men cheered and Durango drew his revolver and fired into the air. Soon he was joined by others, and Warful stepped down from his box, grinning like a skull, to the racket of gunfire and a haze of powder smoke.

Battles stopped the man before he reached his tent.

"I robbed a bank in Pecos and killed a teller," he said.

Warful smiled. "Ah yes, so you did."

"The law will be looking for me."

"Then I suggest you keep your head down and lose yourself in the crowd."

"It's a risk."

"Yes, one you'll have to take, I'm afraid," Warful said. He moved toward his tent. "Now, Marshal, if you'll excuse me."

Battles watched the man go, knowing he was teetering on a knife-edge. Warful didn't trust him, and few of the others did.

He smiled to himself.

His promising career as a lawman could come to a sudden end if he put down one foot wrong—like trying to contact Colonel Sinclair.

Well, San Francisco was a big city and there he'd surely find a way to end this and bring Warful to justice, even if it meant sending a telegraph to Washington for help.

The darkness was drawing close and the night birds were pecking at the first stars. A rising wind sighed through the canyon, tugging at his shirt.

Matt Battles shivered.

Irritated, he realized it might be from fear.

Chapter 14

An Ace in the Hole

The gunmen's horses were saddled and ready to ride before dawn.

Mosey packed up after breakfast. He rode a scrawny mule and led an even scrawnier one, loaded up with pots and pans, the tools of the range cook's trade.

"Bye, boys," he yelled, waving, as he rode out, heading south, the pack mule clanking behind him. "And good luck to all of you."

A few men bade the black man farewell and a couple of others waved.

"Durango," Warful said. He nodded in Mosey's direction.

The gunman returned the nod.

A couple of minutes later he followed Mosey's back trail and a few minutes after that the slam of two shots echoed through the canyon.

The gunmen stood by their horses and a few exchanged glances, but not a voice was raised in protest, the death of a black cook being considered of little account.

Battles watched Durango ride in, horse and rider silhouetted against a bloodred sky, and he gritted his teeth in impotent rage.

He'd witnessed two cold-blooded murders by Durango and had been unable to prevent either.

Standing there in the scarlet-stained morning, the wind cool on his face, Battles vowed that, no matter what happened, he'd make sure Durango didn't live through this affair, even if he had to match his draw against the breed's lightning gun.

A wagon drawn by a pair of mules was parked outside Warful's tent.

The men waited, their horses restless, for Mrs. Hattie Warful to grace the assembled company with her presence.

She didn't disappoint.

Her husband drew back the tent flap with all

the grinning flourish of a master of ceremonies introducing the top banana at a burlesque show.

The lady made her appearance.

She wore heavy makeup, her cheeks and lips the same shade of crimson, and she wore a rustling dress of shimmering green silk.

That the dress covered a filthy, unwashed body did not seem to faze either Mr. or Mrs. Warful in the least. The fat woman scarred the aborning morning by her very presence and polluted the air with her stench.

Warful led his wife to the back of the wagon, looked around for help, met the eyes of no volunteers, and helped her into the bed himself. The springs squealed in protest as Hattie settled her vast bulk, perched on the edge, and kicked her fat legs.

"Are you quite comfy, my love?" Warful said.

The woman frowned. "No, I'm not, Hatfield. I so dread this journey."

"I'll do everything I can to make you comfortable, my dear."

"On the voyage, Hatfield. Will I get seasick?"

"Not at all, my dearest. I'm told a bark of seven hundred tons is an exceptionally smooth-sailing craft."

Hattie pouted, an expression so grotesque, Battles wanted to turn away, but couldn't. He stared at the woman like a rabbit mesmerized by a cobra.

"I don't believe you, Hatfield," she said. "I bet she wallows in the waves like a pig in a trough and makes me sick."

"We'll see, my love," Warful said, even his patience apparently wearing thin.

He tied his horse to the back of the wagon and then climbed into the seat.

"Forward!" he yelled, waving on his gunmen.

Battles mounted with the rest and followed the wagon, one of nineteen expert gunmen who had been lost and then found again.

The marshal glanced around him, at the hard, belligerent faces of the men. Alone, any one of them was a handful. Together, they could stand against an infantry regiment and he wouldn't bet on the outcome.

Could Warful control them once they got to San Francisco, knowing that a fortune in gold was theirs for the taking?

The man must have another ace in the hole that made him so confident.

Battles wished he knew what it was.

Chapter 15

Of Blackjacks and Brass Knuckles

Warful had the men sell their horses in Pecos City, telling them that they'd have no need for them in San Francisco.

A few men who were riding blood horses demurred, including Battles, but Warful soothed their misgivings by pointing out that when they returned to American soil they'd all be riding in carriages.

Battles had to let it go. Now was not the time to make a stand, and not over a horse.

Only Lon Stuart, the dour Texas gunfighter, refused.

"I want my sorrel here, waiting for me, when this business is done," he said. "And I'll kill any man who tries to make me sell him."

Even Warful, crazy as he was, seemed to realize the danger of pushing a man like Stuart. But it was Durango who made up his mind for him. The breed drifted away when the Texan's hard talk started. He didn't want any part of what Stuart could give him.

"Then leave your horse at the livery, Mr. Stuart," Warful said, smiling, smoothing it out. "But, should you need one, you'll find better horseflesh in San Francisco, I assure you."

Stuart shook his head. "There is no better hoss than the sorrel."

"Then do as you please, Mr. Stuart," Warful said. He turned on his heel and walked away, his back stiff.

Stuart looked at Battles. "I don't like that man," he said.

The marshal smiled. "Seems to me, Lon, that men you don't like have a habit of ending up dead."

"Something to bear in mind," the Texan said. His eyes were hard and direct. "Since I don't like lawmen much either."

Battles and the others had Mrs. Warful to thank for the railroad car they had to themselves.

The woman's stench drove the other passengers to seek the less pungent confines of the remaining carriages, while Hattie spread out her bulk over an entire bench.

The restaurant Pullman, with its cushioned seats, was out of bounds for Mrs. Warful because of her great size and odor, and her husband brought her food, an activity that occupied most of his waking hours.

Warful had dropped the Roman salute, which only Durango and a few others used anyway, explaining that it could draw too much attention to themselves.

Battles figured he was right about that. He and

the others would look like a bunch of loons.

In the course of the jolting, sooty, five-day journey to San Francisco, Battles had to change trains four times, a miserable experience that entailed long, tedious waits at stations where the food was bad and the whiskey barely tolerable.

Warful assured his irritable gunmen that better accommodations awaited them in 'Frisco, and that he personally guaranteed their comfort until they took ship.

Even the passing beauty of the Sierra Nevada did little to lift Battles's mood as they neared their destination. Indigestible grub lay in his belly like lead sinkers, and the stink of Mrs. Warful cloyed in his nostrils.

He vowed he would never ride the cushions again, unless it was a journey of an hour or two, and even then it would require some cussin' and discussin' with himself.

The train pulled into San Francisco just before midnight. A heavy mist curled through the streets of the city, and the air was chill and smelled of wet leaves and shoaling fish out in the bay.

"Our accommodations are on the Barbary Coast near the docks," Warful said after he'd gathered the men around him. "I trust Captain Yates has arranged all that."

"Hell, so do I," Dee O'Day said, his shoulders hunched against the cold. Like the others, he had saddlebags slung over his shoulder and carried his long gun.

Warful smiled. "Our host is a gentleman named Shanghai Kelly. He's a rogue and the worst runner in the business, but he keeps a clean place and his cook is a French chef, at least he was until he stuck a boning knife into the chest of a complaining diner and had to flee Boston Town."

"Runner?" Battles said. "Do you mean gun-runner?"

"No, Mr. Battles, I mean there are hell ships out of New York City commanded by captains under whom no seaman in his right mind would sail." Warful flashed his skull grin. "Shanghai Kelly and other runners provide those crews."

"Sounds like a model citizen," Battles said.

"Oh, he is. He's rich now and apparently respectable, but I'm told Shanghai still looks back with fondness on the days when he was reckoned to be the best man with the blackjack, slingshot, and brass knuckles along the entire Barbary Coast."

Warful's attention was drawn to a noise behind him, the clatter and clang of wheels on the cobbles as a cab threaded through traffic toward them.

He stepped into the street and waved down the driver, a man muffled to the ears in an old army greatcoat and woolen scarf, a battered top hat pulled low over his eyes.

"My wife needs transportation to Mr. Kelly's establishment on the coast," he said, looking up at the driver.

The man touched the brim of his hat with his whip.

"Thank'ee, sir," he said. "I'm at your service. He pulled down his muffler and smiled. "As the nun said to the bishop."

"My lady wife is a delicate creature," Warful said. "I fear a walk in this fog might harm her lungs."

"Don't you worry, sir," the driver said. "I'll take care of her gentle, like she was me own missus."

But when the man clapped eyes on Mrs. Warful as she moved out of the shadows, his attitude changed.

He shook his head and said: "Sir, I'd splinter me wheels or kill me horse if I let the lady in question into my cab, beggin' your pardon."

Warful was boiling mad, especially when he noticed most of the gunmen clustered around him were grinning.

"Now, see here, you—" he began.

But he fell silent when a cab heading away from the dock area stopped and the driver, a burly, red-faced man, yelled: "'Ere, are you all right, Charlie?"

"I'm fine, Joe," the first driver said. He slapped the reins and called out over his shoulder as he drove away: "Some folks have no consideration for the tools of a man's livelihood."

After Hattie watched the cab's bobbing orange sidelights disappear into distance and darkness, she let out a wail and Warful ran to his wife's side.

"I can't walk all that distance to the docks, Hatfield," she said. "You know I can't."

"I understand, my love," Warful said. "But there will be another cab by presently."

But none others, perhaps warned by Charlie and Joe, stopped and Mrs. Warful's howls grew in intensity and volume.

A group of Chinese men had stopped to watch this piteous scene; then one stepped forward— and put Hattie out of her misery.

Chapter 16

At the Royal Arms Inn

"We take missy," the man said. "Nice cart. She be comfortable, you see."

Warful was desperate, ready to clutch at any straw.

"Did you hear that, Hattie, my love? We have suitable transportation," he said.

The woman looked uncertain. "But they're Celestials. Might they drive me off somewhere and have their wicked way with me?"

"We'll be right with you, my dear," Warful said. "The Chinese are a perfidious breed to be sure, but they'll behave in the presence of white men."

The Chinese bobbed and smiled.

"Behave? Oh, sure. Missy be safe. Only cost ten dollar."

"That's preposterous," Warful sputtered. "Highway robbery, damn your Chink eyes."

"Ten dollar," the Chinese man insisted. "Missy very large lady."

"For God's sake, pay him, boss," Dee O'Day said. "Or we'll be standing outside this damned station all night."

"Then it's ten dollars," Warful said. "And be damned to you for a thieving Chinaman."

The Chinese man only smiled in return. "Missy enjoy ride. Go slow, enjoy sights."

A two-wheeled cart was produced and four Chinese youths manhandled Mrs. Warful into it. They either didn't mind her smell or they hid their feelings very well.

Watching, Battles decided the latter was the case.

The rickety cart clattering along a cobbled street with a grinning Chinese on each handle and two

76

pushing was an undignified way to travel, and Mrs. Warful gave vent to her feelings, claiming that she was "undone," and "shamed beyond imagining."

As it happened, because of the thick fog that formed pink and blue halos around the gas lamps, few people paid her any heed, as though a fat woman being hauled by four Chinamen was a common sight.

With his far-seeing, frontiersman's eyes, Battles could make out a few of the signs that hung outside the doors of the saloons and brothels lining the street that fronted the Barbary Coast docks: THE ROARING GIMLET, THE COCK OF THE WALK, BULL'S RUN, THE RAMPANT ROOSTER, BELLE OF THE UNION.

There was also one particularly disreputable saloon named the Scarlet Harlot boasted a painted sign that showed a woman in a red dress lying seductively on a bed.

All were doing a roistering business, their gas lamps glazing steamed-up windows with a pale white light.

The misty streets and alleys teemed with roaring people. Sailors, miners, slack-jawed rubes from the hills, doves, pimps, robbers, and cutthroats rubbed elbows and jostled for walking room.

Everywhere he looked, Battles saw an ever-shifting maelstrom of licentiousness, debauchery, misery, grinding poverty, ostentatious wealth, pollution, disease, insanity from bad liquor, dissipation, profanity, blasphemy, and death. Here and there, always alone, pale-faced preachers clutched Bibles to their breasts and warned the few that would listen that hell was yawning open to receive the whole putrid mess.

Of the local constabulary, there was no sign.

By comparison to the other dives, Shanghai Kelly's three-story wooden structure was a model of good taste. The Royal Arms Inn sign showed old Queen Vic in her imperial regalia, obviously not amused as she frowned down at the heaving street.

The bar was busy, but more subdued than others, and Kelly's doves left the premises arm in arm with their clients instead of entertaining them upstairs.

As the Chinese slowed the cart to a stop, the air so close to the bay was even colder, heavy with dampness, and the night smells of oily, stagnant water, filthy ships waiting to be scrubbed out, and the nearby dives were more pungent than polite.

Along the docks a forest of ship masts rose above the curling mist. A listening man could have stopped in his tracks, and, even above the cacophony of pianos and banjo bands, heard the lap, lap, lap of water against wooden hulls and the restless creak of rigging.

. . .

The Chinese, as though to justify their exorbitant fee, helped Mrs. Warful into Kelly's place, an operation that was overseen by the proprietor himself.

Unlike the Celestials, Kelly wore his feelings on his face, and his nose wrinkled when he got close to the fat woman.

"Can she get upstairs by herself?" Kelly said to Warful, eyeing Hattie's enormous bulk.

"No," the man said. "She will need assistance."

He directed a pleading look at a few of his men who were still standing around Kelly's lobby, the others having already made their way to the bar. He found no volunteers.

"We help missy upstairs," a Chinaman said. "Only cost five dollar, by golly."

Warful's anger flared and for a moment Battles thought he'd go for the revolver in his waistband, but Kelly stepped between him and the Chinaman.

He peeled off a five-dollar bill from his thick roll and handed it to the Chinese man. "Room at the top of the stairs. And for God's sake don't drop her. She'll bring the whole place down about our ears."

For a moment it seemed that Warful would direct his anger toward Kelly at this slight to his wife's odorous charms, but he stepped back.

Kelly, who looked like the benign landlord of

an English country pub, was in fact a skull and brass-knuckle street fighter who had killed men with both.

Warful stood in silence as he watched the Chinese successfully carry his wife into her room, and even then he waited until they left before he said: "Is Captain Yates's ship at the docks?"

"Aye, she is," Kelly said, "and on board her the scurviest bunch of rascals as ever sailed the seven seas."

He looked around, then leaned closer to Warful to impart a confidence, which Battles nonetheless overheard.

"His first mate is Mad Dog Donovan."

Warful's face registered shock. "I thought he was hung for a pirate a couple of months back."

"Only half hung. The Dutch botched the job and buried him alive on Sumatra, but Poke dug him up."

"And nursed him back to health?"

"Nursed, hell. A swig of rum and Mad Dog was himself again."

Doubt clouded Warful's face. "Himself again means he'll be barking at the moon. Can we trust him?"

"Trust Mad Dog?" Kelly laughed. "A better question would be, can we trust Poke Yates?"

Chapter 17

A Ravening Sea Wolf

Shanghai Kelly's accommodations were less than luxurious.

He had cots enough for twenty men split among four rooms that were once considered just large enough for a dove and her client.

Battles shared with Dee O'Day, Lon Stuart, a man named Bates he didn't know, and Luke Anderson, a stringbean with the eyes of a lizard who liked doves and was suspected of murdering several.

But the bedding was clean and Kelly had thoughtfully provided chamber pots, one for every two men, a washbasin, and towels.

To everyone's relief, Mrs. Warful shared a room and a brass bed with her husband. The thought of them sleeping together conjured up images in Matt Battles's mind he tried not to dwell upon.

After breakfast on the morning after their arrival, Hatfield Warful took Battles and Durango aside.

"Mr. Battles, I want you to come with me," he said. "Durango, you remain here and keep an eye on things."

The gunman was being worked over by a

hangover and readily agreed to stay behind.

"Hurtin', Durango, huh?" Battles said, grinning.

"You go to hell," the breed said, then winced as the sound of his own voice hammered through his skull.

Warful clucked and shook his head.

"We must all stay sober until this venture is completed, Durango," he said, looking down at the scowling breed from his towering height. "But in the meantime, the sovereign remedy for a hangover is two raw eggs, a shot of brandy, and a generous dash of Tabasco sauce. Mix well and drink."

Durango looked at Warful as though he couldn't believe what he was hearing. His eyes bugged out of his head, and his hand flew to his mouth as his stomach heaved. Then he turned and ran.

"Someday I'll have to do something with that half-breed," Warful said, more to himself than Battles.

"Then you'll have to stand in line," the marshal said.

"My plan is to visit Captain Yates and make sure all arrangements have been made for the loading of the gold," Warful said as he and Battles left the inn and took to the cobbled street that ran parallel to the docks.

The dance halls, concert saloons, and gambling

dives were quiet, drifting in mist, as the Barbary Coast slept after yet another long night of intoxication, fornication, and homicide.

Warful stopped and asked a passing seaman where away lay the bark *Lila*.

The man jerked a thumb over his shoulder. "The square-rigged scow with the eagle figurehead under her bowsprit." The sailor was half drunk and belligerent. He spat at Warful's feet. "And be damned to her and all who sail in her."

The man lurched past, then stopped and turned.

"You tell black Poke Yates that was the hundred and eighth time that Sam Garrety has cursed him and his hell ship."

Battles smiled. "It seems your Captain Yates isn't too popular around these parts."

"All truly great men make enemies, Marshal," Warful said. "That is why I have so many myself."

Matt Battles expected Poke Yates to be a rollicking old seadog with a tarry pigtail and perhaps a cutlass scar or two.

Instead, the man that met him and Warful on the *Lila*'s deck could've been a country parson of the poorest sort.

Yates was small, no more than five foot six and slender, but it was the tough slenderness of a whip, not a weakling.

He wore a black, cutaway Albert coat and pants of the same color, pegged under elastic-sided boots. A boiled white shirt, a four-in-hand tie, and a floppy broad-brimmed hat completed his attire.

His eyes were twinkling blue, full of good humor, but his prissy, steel purse of a mouth suggested that he'd never allowed anyone to crack a dirty joke in his presence or fart in church.

Unfortunately, appearances are deceptive and the very opposite was true.

Poke Yates was a killer with an icy conscience—a relentless pimp and a pirate of opportunity. He was also a first-class ship's captain who had gone to sea as a boy and was a product of Britain's Royal Navy at a time when seamen boasted that they'd joined that harsh service for "rum, bum, and baccy."

Ten years before the mast had hardened Yates and transformed him from orphaned boy into a dangerous, unpredictable man who ruled his ship with an iron fist.

In all, he was a ravening sea wolf in parson's clothing.

Battles stood to one side as Warful and Yates smiled and embraced.

To the marshal it looked as if the gigantic Warful were hugging a child.

Yates stepped back, grinning. "Damn my eyes, but it's good to see you again, Hat," he said. "The Coast has never been the same since the scurvy bastards ran you out on a rail."

"It's good to be back," Warful said. "At the dawn of a great and noble venture."

The two men spoke for a while about old times, and Battles had a chance to look around.

The *Lila* looked as though she was a tight, weatherly craft. Her pine decks were scoured white, all ropes coiled in navy fashion, and Lord Nelson himself would've approved of her rigging and tackle.

But what caught Battles's eye were the two swivel guns attached to the rail of the quarter-deck. Loaded with canister, they could rain death on an unarmed ship—or sweep the *Lila*'s deck clear of boarders.

Or gunfighters.

Seamen, a surly, tough-looking bunch, came and went on the deck as Warful and Yates talked; then Battles was invited into the conversation.

Warful introduced him as a former U.S. Marshal turned bank robber and killer, and Yates seemed impressed by his credentials.

"Good to have you aboard, Mr. Battles," the captain said, shaking hands. "I bet you're anxious to ship out with us."

No other answer coming to mind, Battles said he was.

"Lay to this, we'll need every man jack of ye when we hove to on the African coast," Yates said.

This came as a shock to Battles and for a moment Warful seemed flustered, but then he covered up by saying: "I have not yet told my men of our coming adventure, Captain Yates. I thought I'd wait until the gold was safely aboard and we were at sea."

Yates nodded. "Yes, for safety's sake perhaps that's just as well."

But Battles pushed it as far as he dared.

"We're headed for Africa?" he said. "The other side of the world?"

Warful glanced around him, then at the brightening sky where a few puffy white clouds were drifting inland from the bay.

"Perhaps we should talk in your cabin, Captain Yates," he said finally.

"By all means," Yates said.

Warful looked at Battles. "You are the most intelligent of my mercenaries, and I have much to impart," he said.

Chapter 18

El Dorado

Yates's cabin was as shipshape as his bark, its honey-colored woodwork gleaming from constant polishing.

The furniture consisted of a mahogany desk, decorated with inlaid panels of whalebone, a huge carved Spanish chair, two smaller chairs, and a sleeping berth against an oak bulkhead that separated the captain's cabin from the crew's quarters.

The cabin was relatively small, and smelled of tobacco smoke and rum, overlaid with the distant but foul odor of the as yet only partly scrubbed-out bilges.

Yates waved Battles and Warful into the chairs and sat behind his desk. He picked up a crystal decanter and said: "A glass of rum with ye, gentlemen?"

Warful refused, but Battles accepted, still not recovered from the shock of the captain's mention of Africa.

He'd been on riverboats a few times and hadn't much cared for the experience. A long sea voyage, cooped up with almost a score of temperamental gunmen and a surly crew, promised misery at best and disaster at worst.

Warful watched until Battles had tasted his glass of thick amber Jamaican rum, then said: "Mayhap, Mr. Battles, we should start off by having Captain Yates tell you where this craft is headed after we leave San Francisco."

"Aye, I can do that," Yates said. He took time to light his pipe, then said: "It's a port, a port of call, though there are them who say it's an independent kingdom."

He took the pipe from his mouth, studied the glowing coal, and without looking up said: "The port, or kingdom, call it what you wish, of Eugene de Montijo lies between the Gold Coast and Liberia, like a pimple on the arse of French West Africa."

"A better name for it would be El Dorado," Warful said.

"Indeed," Yates said, nodding, "it is a fabulously wealthy place."

"And ripe for the plucking," Warful said, grabbing air with a clawed hand.

He turned in his chair and said to Battles: "Eugene de Montijo is the center of the African slave trade. The continent is still being bled of its human resources and fifty thousand slaves pass through the kingdom every year, bound for the Arab lands, the rubber plantations of South America and a dozen other nations."

Warful's skull face broke into a smile. "Vast

fortunes are being made, Mr. Battles, millions and millions, and we can take it all by force of arms."

"I thought slavery had been abolished years ago," Battles said, knowing how lame that sounded. But his brain was overwhelmed and couldn't fully process what Warful was telling him.

"Mr. Battles, your naiveté is charming," Warful said, to the bellowing counterpoint of Yates's laughter. "Slavery is still with us, and is growing." He spread his hands and shrugged. "Of course, nowadays when darkies are sent to places like South Africa where slavery is abolished, the British call them 'apprentices.' But the result is the same. Within a few years they're worked to death."

"And you plan to take over this slave trade?" Battles said. He felt sick. But whether it was from the dark rum or Warful's plans, he didn't know.

"Only the Eugene de Montijo part of it," Warful said. "And then there are the Jews, of course. I'll also take care of them."

Suddenly Yates was interested. "What about the Jews, Hat?"

"As you told me yourself, the kingdom suffers from a major infestation," Warful said. "The Jews control the ivory and spice trade and have become very wealthy, and many have huge estates in the hills overlooking the port. I will confiscate those estates and distribute them among my followers." He smiled. "Of necessity, the Jews will have to be exterminated."

Yates picked up the rum decanter, offered it to Battles, who shook his head, then poured himself another glass. "Hat, when I told you about the Jews, I said they were my best customers and that I didn't want them harmed. They ship all over the world and I need their business, lay to that. Most of them are square and I take to them like pitch, I do."

"You will have plenty of other business, I promise you," Warful said, dismissing the man. "One day all the nations of earth will get rid of the Jewish problem. Until then, the world will see the pogrom at Eugene de Montijo as a start."

Battles detected a shift in the captain's attitude and there was an edge of hostility in his voice as he said: "You plan to storm the palace and overthrow King Brukwe with a score of men?"

"Yes, those, and the five hundred mounted Afrikaner mercenaries your man Marcel Toucey is bringing north."

"The trouble with Toucey is that he's a rogue who should've been hung years ago," Yates said. "You can't depend on him. And you can't depend on the Boers either. The last I heard, they're planning a major armed revolt against the British. If that's the case, they'll want all their fighting men at home."

"Why are sailors such pessimists?" Warful said, smiling. "In the unlikely event that the Afrikaners don't arrive, I can take the palace with my gunfighters and your crew."

"Hat, King Brukwe has two hundred soldiers and his personal bodyguard consists of fifty Amazons he calls the Iron Handmaidens," Yates said. "His women can use weapons better than any men and they're vicious. They're so dedicated to Brukwe that once in a while a Handmaiden will kill herself on his order, to prove the loyalty of the others."

Warful opened his mouth to speak, but the captain held up a hand for silence.

"The king's soldiers are armed with British Martini-Henry rifles and a couple of Gatling guns," Yates said. "The French gave them two cannons that they've learned to shoot fairly well."

Yates sat back in his chair and talked over steepled fingers. "Taking over the kingdom won't be as easy as you think." He smiled faintly. "And King Brukwe likes his Jews."

Warful was irritated and it showed.

"Damn it, Poke," he said, dropping his previous formality, "your attitude has changed since the last time we spoke. Once you were all for conquering the kingdom and taking over the slave trade. What's changed your mind?"

"Well, Hat, the French for one thing," Yates said. "They abolished slavery in 1848 under the Second Republic and—"

The captain cocked his head on one side like an inquisitive bird. "You know Smiling Jack Rawlings, master of the clipper *Lady Clare*?"

"I know him," Warful said. The man was on a slow burn.

"Smiling Jack just returned from the Gold Coast and he says the talk is that the French plan to take over Eugene de Montijo, throw King Brukwe out on his ear, and hang all the slave traders."

"It's talk, just talk," Warful said. "The French reap taxes from the kingdom, and the English and Dutch make money. They'll leave it alone."

Yates looked at Battles. "Is he to be trusted?"

"No," Warful said.

"Well, I'll say my piece anyhow."

Yates stabbed a forefinger at Warful. "Hat, forget Africa. That plan has gone all to hell. Here's what I want you to do—pay off your gunmen and send them home. After the gold is loaded we'll sail the *Lila* to Old Mexico and sell the booty to the Diaz government at five times the American price."

"And what do I get out of it, Poke?" Warful said, his eyes cold.

"I owe you a favor or three from the old days, Hat. You'll get a first mate's share, square and true, lay to that. Enough to keep you and your lady wife in luxury for the rest of your days."

"Hell, Poke, you're talking like an old lady," Warful said. "If Africa scares you so much, why not just take the gold to the Indian prince and be done with it?"

"No," Yates said. "This is the biggest score of my life. After I pay off, I'll sell the *Lila* and retire from the sea. I'm not getting any younger, Hat, and the hard years are catching up with me. It's time I laid up in a cozy berth, permanent like, with bacon and eggs for breakfast and a willin' woman at my side."

The captain's face hardened. "As to being a frightened old lady, I'll meet you on my deck with pistols or a cutlass any damn time you choose."

Battles expected Warful to explode, but to his surprise the man merely smiled, his eyes shining, and said: "Yes, I spoke out of turn, Poke. But you're passing up millions, the chance to live like an English lord, and those of your blood that come after you as well."

"Maybe what you say is true, but the risk is too great. We could all end up hanging from a French noose. Savvy?"

Warful nodded. "Yes, then we'll play it your

way. Once the gold is loaded, we'll set a course for Old Mexico."

Yates rose to his feet, smiling, and extended his hand. "Then put it there, shipmate. You've made a wise decision to sail close to the wind."

Warful shook the captain's hand warmly.

But his eyes were again the color of bleach.

Chapter 19

Brass Buttons for a Mad Dog

Matt Battles walked onto the dock with a silent, seething Warful striding beside him.

They were about to cross the street, busy at that time of the morning with delivery wagons of all kinds, significant among them huge beer drays and their straining, four-horse teams, but Warful stopped and turned to Battles. The giant's hands were trembling and now his eyes were filled with an unholy fire.

"So Poke wants a cozy berth," he said. "Well, by God, I'll give him one—a tight pine box six feet under the sod."

Battles smiled. "You didn't think much of his proposition, huh?"

"Did you?"

"It beats hanging."

"The French will hang nobody," Warful said. "Politicians in Paris can poke holes in the air with their fingers and talk about the evils of slavery, but their officials in Africa are getting rich off the trade."

Warful bent his head, talking closer to the marshal's ear. "We'll kick King Brukwe out on his black ass, take over the kingdom, and the Frogs won't even raise an eyebrow."

Battles hedged, unwilling to show his hand. "Why not pay off your men and take Yates's deal?"

"Because I want a kingdom," Warful said, his eyes distant. "It is my birthright and I will rule wisely and well in a land free of the Jewish pestilence and where Negroes live in slavery, as is their birthright."

The man was as mad as a hatter and Battles decided there and then that the *Lila* must not be allowed to leave San Francisco.

Somehow he had to make his break and talk to the city police.

It wasn't going to be easy.

"Hatfield Warful, look at me, poor Mad Dog Donovan, as ever was."

Battles saw a tall, thin man coming toward them, moving with a strange bird-hop gait.

"Mr. Donovan," Warful said, smiling, "Captain Yates told me you'd been half hung since last we met."

Donovan spat. "The Dutchies, damn them.

Hung me for a pirate rogue, and me as square as the driven snow."

Warful turned to Battles. "You've heard me talk of Mr. Donovan, the one they call Mad Dog."

"Aye, Mad Dog is my name," Donovan said. A sly look came into his black eyes. "But I can tell a sailor from a sundial, any day of the month. Says you, 'Never was truer words spoke and by a finer seaman.'"

"You have a way with you, right enough," Warful said.

"And I ain't got much time for fools, me bein' as smart as new paint as you're well aware," Donovan said.

The first mate of the *Lila* wore a claw-hammer coat over a striped jersey and washed-out canvas pants that had once been a blue color. A red bandanna was tied around his head and at the base of his neck. He was missing his left hand. In its place was a smooth chunk of bullet-shaped ivory, inlaid with an exquisitely wrought Chinese dragon in green jade, two scarlet rubies for its eyes.

"I seen ye talking to Sam Garrety, Cap'n Warful," he said. "What was that lubberly seaman telling you?"

Warful smiled. "He just cursed the *Lila* and all who sail in her."

"For the one hundred and eighth time," Battles said.

"Aye, he'd do that, damn his eyes," Donovan said. "He's never forgotten the day I tickled his back with the cat fer pilfering rum. Thirty strokes o' the best I gave him, and him squealing like a birthing sow the whole time. Says you, 'You done your duty, Mr. Donovan. The cat speaks every language in the world, it does, with its nine tongues.'"

"There's no evil in skinning a thief's back," Warful said.

Donovan looked sly again. "D'ye smell it, lads?"

"Smell what?" Warful said.

"There's blood on the wind, and the stink of hammered iron festering in a man's guts."

"I don't smell blood," Warful said.

"Not yet, ye don't, Cap'n. But ye will, lay to that."

Donovan tipped his head to one side and stared hard into Warful's eyes.

"Bound fer Africa, are ye not?" Mad Dog did a little jig. "Weigh anchor and hoist the mizzen, I say, and let's around the Horn."

He took a step back, pointed his ivory stump at Warful, and laughed, the high-pitched cackle of a madman. "Them Africans will kill you, Cap'n. They'll shove a pointed stick up your ass."

The slightly contemptuous, faintly amused expression on Warful's face didn't change.

"Will you sail us to Africa, Mr. Donovan?" he said.

"Ah, and for why? says Mad Dog."

"I'll make you the captain of the *Lila*."

The man's face brightened. "You'll give me a blue coat with brass buttons and a spyglass a yard long?"

"Of course. Every captain should have those things."

"Then I'm your man."

"I may have to get rid of Captain Yates, mind," Warful said.

"Then cut his throat, says I, and be done with him."

"I thought the man saved your life," Battles said.

Donovan nodded. "That he did. He brought me back from the dead."

His next words cut through the morning air like a knife.

"He did me no favor. Soon he'll know that Mad Dog was better left in the grave."

Chapter 20

Treasure!

Warful warned Matt Battles to keep his mouth shut about what had been said at his meeting with Poke Yates.

"I'll tell the men what's happening, but only after we've cleared the straits and are at sea," he said.

Battles pretended indifference. "You're the boss," he said.

An hour later Warful called a meeting of his hungover gunmen, filling a room at the back of his premises that Kelly kept for private conferences.

Warful glanced around the assembled men, then said: "Now that we've all gathered, I have something to tell you that you will be glad you heard."

Warful beamed like a benign schoolmaster, then said: "The gold will be loaded into the *Lila* the day after tomorrow. After that is completed, I plan to capture the ship and take possession of its cargo."

"Now you're talking, boss," Dee O'Day yelled. "Gun the crew an' take the gold, like I always said."

"No, Mr. O'Day," Warful said. "That much

gunfire would certainly draw the attention of the police, even on the Barbary Coast."

"Then we cut their throats, quietlike, and sail to somewhere and divide the take," O'Day said.

"Have you ever sailed a ship, Mr. O'Day?" Warful said. His eyes traveled over his men. "Have any of you ever sailed a ship?"

Getting no answer, he said: "Without the sailors we wouldn't even be able to leave port."

"Then, damn it, who do I kill?" O'Day said. "Give me a name."

"The captain will be deposed," Warful said. "But only the captain. We need the seamen alive."

Lon Stuart's eyes looked like chips of flint and his dour stare telegraphed his irritation.

"So we have the gold and the boat," he said. "Then what?"

"I'll tell you all when we're at sea," Warful said.

When a man who is good with a gun moves his hand a fraction of an inch closer to his holstered iron, alarm bells ring.

And those bells clamored in Warful's eyes big-time when Stuart dropped his hand slightly and said: "No, you'll tell us now."

The gunmen mumbled their agreement and Sam Thorne, a fast gun who was just as dour and dangerous as Stuart, said: "Damn right you will."

Battles studied Warful's stricken face. The man had very suddenly run out of room on the dance floor and was in danger of losing his hold over his gunmen.

For a few long, ticking moments, the situation balanced on a knife-edge, but the tall man rose to the occasion.

Warful spread out his arms and adopted a suffering expression, as though he was crucified by their doubt.

"Do you want me to tell all, reveal my most closely guarded secrets?" he called out, like a man in extremis.

"Yeah, we do," Thorne said, the knife scar on his left cheek bone white against his flushed face. "That's the way of it."

"Treasure!" Warful screamed.

He let the ensuing silence stretch, then said: "Gold, diamonds, rubies, the finest pearls in all creation, crowns, diadems, necklaces, rings, riches stacked as high as a tall man. A king's ransom, nay, not a king, the ransom of an 'undred mighty emperors!"

A murmur of interest ran through the gunmen, and even Battles was intrigued. Neither Poke Yates nor Warful had mentioned treasure before.

"We have a treasure right out there at the docks," Stuart said. "Why hunt for more?"

"Because the gold we have is nothing

compared to the fabulous wealth that lies within our grasp," Warful said.

Greed is a spur that goads a man to recklessness, and by nature, every man in the room heeded the siren song of easy money.

"Where is this treasure, boss?" Dee O'Day said.

Warful let the tension build for a few moments, then said: "Africa!"

O'Day stepped into the brooding silence that followed this announcement.

"Where the hell is that?" he said.

"East, Mr. O'Day, to a slave port named Eugene de Montijo, a city bursting with all the riches of the world."

"And where the hell is the treasure?" a gunman said.

"Ah, a good question. The treasure lies in the palace strongroom of the local king, guarded by a few dozen of his men." Warful grinned. "We can take it from him and be back on board the *Lila* with the treasure within an hour."

"How long does it take to sail to this . . . Africa place?" O'Day asked.

"No more than forty days or even less, depending on the trade winds," Warful said. "The *Lila* is the fastest bark on the high seas, mind."

"Forty days at sea is a long time for landsmen like us," Stuart said.

"Indeed it is," Warful said. "But it's a small investment of your time that will pay off in great riches. You will all return to the United States fabulously wealthy men."

Warful looked around the room. "Well, what say you men, will you come with me?"

"You sure about that forty days?" Stuart said before anyone could answer.

"Indeed I am," Warful said. "Why, it's little more than a month. Most of you have spent that amount of time in a brothel without even noticing it."

The tall man got a few laughs, but they were subdued, wary.

Stuart's eyes were moving from one man to the next. He saw no real expressions of dissent.

"All right, boss, we'll play it your way," he said. "But if it goes bad, for any reason, we turn around, fog it back to the good ol' U.S. of A. and keep the gold we have."

Warful nodded. "You can't say fairer than that, Mr. Stuart. As soon as the gold is loaded, we take the ship, then sail for . . ." His voice rose to a shout. "Africa!"

Battles noted that the response was less than enthusiastic, but for now the gunmen would go along with Warful's plan, the lure of vast wealth overcoming their better judgment.

After a few days riding the rollers of the Pacific, they just might change their minds.

After the meeting broke up, Battles took Warful aside.

"You lied about the treasure, didn't you?" he said.

Warful shrugged. "Who's to say that King Brukwe doesn't have a treasure?"

"If he doesn't, the men won't fight to put you on his throne."

"Oh, but they will, Mr. Battles," Warful said. "They will have to—or die."

Chapter 21

A Great Secret

Later that morning, Matt Battles stuck his Colt in his waistband and headed for the door. Warful, who seemed to have eyes in the back of his head, stepped out of the bar area and called out to him.

"Taking a walk, Mr. Battles?" he said.

"I need to stretch my legs and get some fresh air," Battles said. "I figure to walk around town a little, see the sights."

"An excellent idea. I'm afraid there will be little opportunity for walking aboard ship."

Warful stepped to the door of the barroom and stuck his head inside. "Mr. O'Day, Durango, can you come here?"

When the two gunmen appeared, Warful said: "Mr. Battles says he's in need of a walk and I'd like you men to accompany him."

Durango grinned. "Hold his hand, you mean?"

"Alas, the Barbary Coast is a dangerous place for a man walking alone. Footpads and cutthroats of every stripe are always on the scout for the unwary."

"I don't need company," Battles said.

Damn it, this was not going as he planned.

"Ah, but I insist," Warful said. He smiled like a snake. "Even the police avoid the Coast, so they'd probably be unable to come to your assistance should you land in trouble."

Disappointment sank in Battles's belly like a lead weight. He realized that Warful guessed what he'd been planning and he wasn't about to allow him out of his sight—even if it was through the bleary eyes of Durango and O'Day.

With two gunmen shadowing his every move, Battles had no chance of going to the police.

O'Day, a killer with the intelligence of a ten-year-old, didn't know what was happening. But Durango did, and there was a triumphant lilt to the man's grin.

Battles nodded. "Very considerate of you," he said to Warful. "I wasn't aware of the dangers."

"You'll be quite safe with Mr. O'Day and Durango, I assure you," the man said. "They're both skilled with arms and dead shots."

That last was a warning, and Battles accepted it as such.

He smiled at Durango. "You ready to do some walking?"

Durango and O'Day were former cowboys and shared the puncher's distaste for walking any distance. They also had the cowboy's love of tight, foot-pinching boots with two-inch heels, made for riding a horse, not trudging the cobbled streets and alleys of a crowded city.

Battles, who had slipped into the pair of Ute moccasins he always carried in his saddlebags, set a punishing pace.

The devil in him, he walked briskly past saloons and dance halls that were still being swamped and had few customers. He wheeled suddenly into crowded alleys where small Chinese men scurried past, each carrying heavy burdens on the ends of a supple, bamboo pole slung across a shoulder. Others balanced huge bundles of soiled clothing and sheets on their heads. None spared a glance for Battles as they trotted past, chattering to one another in a language he could not understand.

After an hour of this, Battles saw to his joy that both O'Day and Durango were hobbling, grimacing in pain as their custom-made boots pinched and scoured the skin of their heels raw.

Finally, when he saw that Battles had no intention of stopping, Durango yelled to him: "Damn you, Matt, take another step and I swear, I'll put a bullet into your back."

Battles stopped and looked back, grinning. "You're not a walking man, huh, Durango?"

"Get the hell back to Kelly's place," the gunman said. "Your walking is done."

O'Day sat on the cobbles and fetched his back against a wall. He pulled off his boots and said: "I'm walking back in my sock feet."

"Your tootsies hurt, Dee?" Battles said, his face empty.

O'Day's hand dropped to his holstered Colt. "Don't tempt me, Battles," he said. "Just . . . don't . . . tempt . . . me."

The marshal grinned. "I'd better get you boys home, I guess."

As Battles preceded his hobbling, cursing companions into Kelly's inn, he noticed that a small steam crane had been maneuvered into position on the docks, close to the *Lila*.

Poke Yates was on the deck, talking to a couple of workmen, and Battles surmised he was instructing them on how to lower the gold into his ship's hold.

The marshal knew he was running out of time, and, closely watched as he was, his chances of getting to the police were growing slimmer with every passing hour.

. . .

The day was shaded into night and the Barbary Coast roused itself and painted its face like a tired old dove ready for another night of debauchery.

Warful stopped Battles, who was on his way to the dining room.

"Enjoy your walk, Marshal?" he said.

The word "marshal" was carefully chosen. Battles was under suspicion and Warful let him know it.

"Yeah," he said, "I enjoyed it. I don't know about my guards, though."

Warful feigned surprise. "Guards? Oh, dear no. Let's say companions." His mouth stretched in a yellow grin. "I'm afraid Mr. O'Day and Durango are in considerable distress. Mr. O'Day can't get his boots on, and Durango can't get his off."

"Sorry to hear that," Battles said.

His eyes moved to the plates Warful was holding. One was piled high with roast beef, potatoes, and creamed onions. The other supported a huge wedge of apple pie.

"For my lady wife, you understand," Warful said. "She is a delicate creature and quite unable to grace the dining room with her presence."

He leaned closer, as though about to impart a great secret.

"She's begun to harbor the most singular

fancies," Warful said. "She says that when I conquer Eugene de Montijo I must cut the finger off a Jewess and bring her the wedding ring." The man smiled. "Such fancies! I hope she's not in . . . what shall I say . . . a certain condition."

Battles smiled and nodded. *Oh God, so do I.*

"Ah well," Warful said, "time will tell."

That night a hired thug from the waterfront was placed outside Battles's room and several more were posted in the street.

Warful said it was for his own protection, since there were rogues along the Coast that might remember him when he was a marshal and could seek revenge for past grievances.

But Battles was now a prisoner and he couldn't understand why Warful kept him around. But the man was devious and probably had other plans for him.

As to what those might be, he had no idea.

Chapter 22

The Death of a Captain

The gold, packed in kegs as Warful said it would be, was loaded the next day and the work continued until early evening.

Warful gathered his men around him and waited until the last keg was on board.

"Now we make our move," he said. "And you men leave Poke Yates to me."

Warful led his men across Pacific Street to the dock, drawing no attention from the pleasure-seekers who were already crowding into the saloons and dance halls.

Mad Dog Donovan stood in shadow by the steam crane and called out to Warful by name.

Warful greeted him and said: "Is all ready?"

Mad Dog nodded. "The gold is stowed safe and sound and the captain is in his cabin." The man leaned closer to Warful and whispered: "There's a breeze blowing fair for the Golden Gate and he plans to sail with the night tide."

"Did he intend to inform me?" Warful said.

Donovan shook his head. "You didn't enter into his talk, or his thinking. Says you, 'Ol' Poke planned to weigh anchor and wave good-bye to me from his quarterdeck.'"

"Damn Yates for a black-hearted rogue," Warful said. "I knew I smelled treachery in the wind."

"How about the sailors?" Durango said. "Will they fight to save their captain?"

"I spoke to all hands, and every man jack of them agreed that Poke is a hard master who has scarred the backs of too many lively sailor lads," Donovan said. "They say they'll accept Mad Dog as master, as long as I'm free with the rum and beer and sparing of the lash."

"Then let's get it done," Warful said.

"Wait, Cap'n Warful," Donovan said. "What about my coat?"

"When we reach Africa, Captain Donovan, I'll get you a blue coat with the finest brass buttons, never fear."

Mad Dog nodded and looked sly. "I know a sailor from a sundial, don't I?"

"Yes, you do," Warful said. "You're as sharp as a tack. I saw that when I first set eyes on you."

"Then take this." Donovan opened his coat and slid a cutlass from its scabbard. "The coppers know we've gold on board, and gunshots could draw their attention." He grinned, revealing few teeth and those black. "Ram this blade through ol' Poke's guts, quietlike. Says you, 'That'll take the life out of him, sure enough.'"

Warful took the cutlass.

"Mr. Battles, you will stay with me," he said. "The rest of you will remain on deck and keep the sailors honest. Durango, secure the swivel guns, but no shooting. Captain Donovan is right. We don't want gunshots to draw the attention of any passing police."

Suddenly the cutlass flickered upward and Warful laid the keen edge against Battles's throat.

Without taking his eyes from the marshal, Warful said: "Durango, relieve Mr. Battles of his firearm."

Battles's hand moved to his Colt, but the edge of the cutlass dug deeper.

"I wouldn't," Warful said. "Not unless you want your throat cut."

"Damn it," Lon Stuart said. "Is he with us or against us?"

"I don't know," Warful said, "but I'm not taking any chances. He could fire shots to signal the plods."

Durango reached down and lifted the revolver from Battles's waistband.

"Your weapon will be returned to you when we're at sea," Warful said. He smiled and flicked the cutlass blade away. "No hard feelings, Mr. Battles. I hope we are still perfect friends."

"No hard feelings," the marshal said. The taste of defeat was like bitter bile in his mouth.

Mad Dog Donovan led the way on deck. The *Lila's* crew had gathered near the forward shrouds, their faces set and grim, and Warful ordered his gunmen to deploy in a line facing them.

Donovan had assured Warful that the sailors were ready for a change of captain, but it seemed to Battles that the bark was a powder keg with a dangerously short fuse.

The twenty-five crewmen carried no firearms, but a few had cutlasses at their sides and others had foot-long marlin spikes or belaying pins shoved into the waistbands of their canvas pants.

Warful said something to Durango, and the breed, O'Day, and a few others mounted the stairs to the quarterdeck and trained the swivel guns on the crew.

A surge of angry talk ran through the seamen, and the gunmen skinned their revolvers. Lon Stuart, careful-eyed and dangerous, stepped to one side, the palm of his left hand over the hammer of his Colt, ready to fan death into the massed sailors.

Warful saw the menace building and threw up his hands, his voice rising. "No one need die today," he said. "Put away your weapons."

Donovan stepped between the edgy crew and the edgier gunmen.

"You men heard Mr. Warful," he said. "Be about your duties and ready the *Lila* for sea, you lubbers. We sail with the tide."

None of the men on either side made a move.

But then Poke Yates stepped onto the deck and in an instant everything changed.

Warful knew the time for talking was done. Only fast, conclusive action would decide the issue.

The last words uttered by Captain Yates to end the final chapter of his life were "What the hell is—"

The cutlass that rammed through his belly,

driven by the full force of Hatfield Warful's considerable strength, robbed him of further speech.

Yates couldn't even find the breath to scream, but he had time enough to die hard.

"You're relieved of duty, Captain," Warful said, looking down at the man lying on his back on the deck, the cutlass sticking upward, out of him, like a skewer in a bloody piece of meat.

Yates's eyes were wide, accusing, outraged at the time and manner of his dying. He opened his mouth to speak, but blood filled his mouth, darkness filled his eyes, and death took the old pirate by the ear and dragged him away.

Warful pulled the cutlass from Yates's body, held the bloody blade high, and yelled: "Huzzah for Captain Donovan, the new master of the *Lila*."

There were no answering cheers. A few hands stepped over and looked at Yates, then turned away, shaking their heads.

They had no love for their former captain and had witnessed assassinations change masters before, but Mad Dog Donovan would not have been their choice, and the presence of the gunmen rankled.

Matt Battles watched the faces of the crew as they dispersed and began to ready the *Lila* for sea. To a man, they were sullen and angry. Sailors whose orderly world had suddenly been turned upside down by force had mutinied for less.

Battles stared into the crystal ball of his consciousness and foresaw disaster. More blood would run red on the decks ere this voyage was over.

Chapter 23

A Terrible Warning

The delicate matter of getting Hattie Warful aboard the *Lila* was solved when Donovan organized a makeshift winch to hoist her on board.

She was immediately assisted to the captain's cabin by her husband, amid mutterings of how unlucky it was to have a woman on ship, especially one that smelled worse than the bilges of an Arab slaver dhow.

Aided by a fair wind and a following sea, *Lila* slipped away from the dock and made excellent speed to the Golden Gate.

The green sea shaded to cobalt blue as the ship sailed through the Gate and breasted the first of the Pacific's rolling breakers.

It was then that Warful dragged Yates's body to the rail and unceremoniously pitched it overboard.

The sailors watched but said nothing.

Donovan ordered a course to the south, and

then sent hands aloft to spread every inch of canvas. The *Lila*'s topgallants filled with wind as she bent to her task.

The bark was a fine ship and Mad Dog, for all his insanity, knew his business and handled her well.

A square-rigged bark is a beautiful ship and, under a full moon, the *Lila* glided across the Pacific like an evening swan.

The man at the helm, humming to himself as he intently watched the luff of the sails, was an army deserter by the name of Judah Rawlings. A former cavalry trooper, Rawlings was small, thin, with the intelligent, inquisitive face of a rodent.

"How are they?" he said, when Battles joined him on the quarterdeck.

"Sick, every last one of them. I couldn't stand the stink of puke, so I came up on deck." He breathed deeply. "Ah, the sea air smells good."

"Aye," Rawlings said, "the smell of the sea lingers in a man's memory long after his footprints in the sand are gone."

Battles looked off the port side of the ship and saw lights in the distance. "Where is that?" he said, nodding.

"Old Mexico, I reckon," the seaman said. "The trade wind blows from the north, and that's why we're making good speed. Once we're off the coast of South America, we'll tack into a south wind."

He smiled. "Your shipmates down below are going to feel a lot worse before they feel better. You're lucky."

"The good Lord didn't make me handsome or especially smart, but he did give me a cast-iron stomach," Battles said.

"You'll need it on this voyage," Rawlings said. "A steady diet of salt pork, salt beef, an' duff ain't for the delicate."

A companionable silence stretched between the two men, the only sound the creak of rigging and the soft spatter of sea spray when the *Lila* dipped her bowsprit.

After a while Rawlings said: "You same as them down below, one o' them Texas draw fighters everybody talks about?"

"I'm nothing like them," Battles said.

"Maybe so. You're a watching man, though," Rawlings said. "You're a rough and ready hand, but square right enough, I reckon, Mr. . . ."

"Name's Matt Battles."

"Then it's Matt and Judah, between us, like?"

"That will work just fine."

The haloed moon rode high in the sky and laid a silver road across the sea for shoaling fish to follow. The air was cool, tangy with salt, and it gently fanned Battles's cheeks, softly, like the eyelashes of a pretty woman.

His eyes reaching into the darkness ahead, his hands steady on the wheel, Rawlings said without turning: "He didn't look it, but the roughest hand to ever sail into the port of San Francisco was Poke Yates."

"He looked like a preacher," Battles said.

"Aye, and maybe that will serve him well in hell, though he cut many a spry sailorman to pork collops with the cutlass or lash and he'll be held to account for that, and worse."

Battles smiled. "Will you miss him, Judah?"

"Not a bit. But you take Mad Dog, now. He's a jolly enough rogue an' no mistake, free with the rum and second go's o' duff, but he's never a ship's captain."

Remembering Rawlings's term, Battles said: "Is he square?"

The seaman didn't answer for a while, and when he did he came at his reply from an angle.

"I've taken to ye, Matt, so I'll tell you a secret," he said. "Did ye hear the ships bell that just rang?"

Battles allowed that he had.

"Six bells. That means we're three hours into the first watch. A man with a clock would see the time as eleven at night."

"Sounds about right, I guess," Battles said, wondering where the hell this was leading.

"Tomorrow night, listen for them six bells."

"So I'll know the time?"

"No, mate, so you'll know there's mischief afoot, the kind that leaves tall Texas men like you a-dying on the deck with their throats cut."

"You mean Mad Dog will try something?"

"I mean only what I says. And you should say, 'Judah Rawlings doesn't want a madman as a captain, so I should heed his warning.'"

The helmsman looked around him warily, then added: "'Judah will tell me no more, says you, so for now I'll let sleeping dogs lie, especially mad ones.'"

It was clear to Battles that Mad Dog Donovan wasn't as crazy as he made out. Certainly he was sane enough to plan a massacre and then take the gold stowed in the cargo hold for himself.

The *Lila* could tie up at a Mexican or South American port, sell the gold to the highest bidder, and Donovan would live high on the hog for the rest of his life.

Battles hadn't seen Warful since they'd boarded, and by now the man was probably as seasick as the rest.

He stepped down to the deck, Rawlings studiously ignoring him, and prepared himself to go below again, into the stinking charnel house where a score of gunmen lay puking their guts out.

He needed them on their feet and prepared to fight.

It was already tomorrow, and the night's six bells would come soon enough.

Battles had little time to head off a massacre.

Chapter 24

Council of War

Matt Battles's efforts to rouse the sick gunmen were met with groans and curses. Dee O'Day, green to the gills, told the marshal to let him die in peace and Lon Stuart, who always seemed indestructible, was bent over, his body racked by dry heaves.

Only one man looked fairly well, John Tidy, a bank and train robber of some reputation who had learned his profession under the tutelage of Jesse and Frank James.

Tidy sat at a mess table and was trying to keep down a cup of water. Around him, snoring sailors swung in eighteen-inch-wide hammocks, oblivious to the stench of vomit, sweat, and stale tobacco.

The ship rolled constantly in the sweeping Pacific waves, and Battles staggered over prone bodies and half fell onto the bench opposite Tidy.

The outlaw looked at him with a bloodshot stare that showed no interest and little friendliness.

"How do you feel, John?" Battles said.

The man was surly. "What do you think, lawman? And why the hell do you care?"

"I need to talk to you," Battles said. "Not here.

On deck where there's fresh air. I need you alert."

"Go to hell," Tidy said. He puffed his cheeks as a wave of nausea hit him.

"John, do you want to die?" Battles said.

The outlaw nodded. "Right now? Yeah, I do. Gladly."

"By this time tonight, you and the rest of these men will be dead," Battles said. "I mean, from a cut throat, not the seasickness."

Tidy's eyes looked like piss holes in snow.

"What the hell are you talking about, Battles?" he said.

"Mad Dog Donovan intends to kill us all and keep the gold for himself," Battles said. "Did I say it plain enough for you?"

Tidy glared at the marshal for a long time, trying to gauge his sincerity. He made up his mind. "Help me up the damned ladder and we'll talk. But if you're acting like an old maid hearing a rustle in the bushes, Battles, I'll gun you fer sure."

The trade wind was still blowing fair from the north, and the *Lila*'s sails billowed as she headed south past the Mexican headlands at a spanking speed. The moon, still as bright as a coin, now hung lower in the sky and silvered the ship's wake.

The fresh air of the weather deck helped Tidy

and he listened intently, his hand on the starboard rail, as Battles recounted his conversation with the helmsman.

"You heard him right?" Tidy said. "Maybe he was lying."

"Yes, I heard him right," Battles said. "And he wasn't lying. After all my years as a peace officer, I usually can tell when a man is spinning a windy."

"Then you reckon we're in for a fight."

"Or a massacre, if we can't get the men on their feet."

"Have you told Warful?"

"No, not yet. I reckon he's probably as sick as the rest."

Tidy thought for a while, then said: "You and me could go after Donovan, gun the son of a bitch."

"His cabin is forward, and he'll be well guarded," Battles said. "Only half the crew are in their hammocks. He'll keep the rest close."

Tidy gave Battles a rare smile, like ice breaking in a pond.

"I'm in the mood for a fight," he said. "Let Mad Dog and his jack-tars have at it."

Battles's eyes reached into the darkness. "They'll come from the front of the ship," he said. "Up there on the quarterdeck, there's a couple of swivel guns, the sailors call them smashers, and we'll need to man those."

"Ben Lane and Luke Anderson both handled cannon during the war," Tidy said. "Anderson is a demon when he's around women, but he's rock steady in a gunfight."

"Good. Then tonight we'll use the darkness to get all the men on deck and Lane and Anderson on the swivel guns," Battles said. "Just before six bells on the first watch, Donovan will call his seamen forward and arm them."

"What about the ranny who steers the boat and told you about Donovan's plan?" Tidy said.

"He says he's on our side, but I'll keep an eye on him just the same."

"Then let's get the boys on their feet and tell them what's happening," Tidy said. "We'll also need to tell Warful."

Battles's teeth gleamed white in the gloom. "Do you want to open the door of his cabin?"

"Hell no," Tidy said, shuddering.

A man suffering from seasickness, even the hardest hard case, sets all pride and ego aside and wishes only to die, and the sooner the better. Thus he becomes a captive, if inattentive, audience.

There was no question of talking to the gunmen with a full watch of seamen in their hammocks. The sailors all seemed to be asleep, but ears may be open, even though eyes are closed.

A wooden partition with a single door

separated the seamen's quarters from a small galley. Beyond this, screened by only a canvas tarp, was an open hatch and ladder that led down to the orlop, the lowest deck on the ship.

Battles took a lantern from the galley and descended the ladder. He found himself in a low-beamed deck filled with spare ropes and cables, and there was a brand-new sea anchor stowed amidships.

After a last look around, Battles climbed the ladder again and found Tidy waiting for him at the hatch.

"Well?" he said.

"We'll go down there where it's private and try to get the men on their feet," Battles said.

"All of them?" Tidy said, surprised.

"No, not at first. We'll start with Lon Stuart and Durango."

Tidy whistled between his teeth. "Ol' Lon is liable to start shooting if we try to move him."

"That's a chance we'll have to take," Battles said. "Get his gun from him if you can. And do the same with Durango."

"You like to live dangerously, don't you, lawman?" Tidy said, shaking his head.

"That's nothing to the danger we'll be in if we don't get those two bad men upright," Battles said.

Chapter 25

Matt Battles Takes a Hand

Sick as they were, and apart from a tirade of cursing, Stuart and Durango put up little resistance and Tidy's deft removal of their guns drew their teeth.

Once in the shifting, lamp-splashed gloom of the orlop, Battles forced both men to sip water while Tidy stood guard at the hatch.

Stuart and Durango were covered in vomit, theirs and other men's, and they smelled to high heaven.

Durango pulled himself together enough to look around, his bloated face puzzled. "What the hell are we doing down here?" he said.

"I need to talk to you, both of you," Battles said. "Are you well enough to listen?"

Stuart, irritated, turned to Durango and said: "We're dying, and the son of a bitch is asking us conundrums."

"You'll die a heap faster if you don't hear what I have to say."

Battles looked at Tidy, who was standing on the ladder, his head bent, listening.

"All right up there?" Battles said.

Tidy stuck his head through the hatch, then ducked back and gave the all-clear.

Battles again turned his attention to Stuart and Durango.

"I'm going to tell you something," he said. "And I want you to listen."

"Hell, man, we're sick," Durango said.

"There can't be any puke left inside you to throw up," Battles said. "Drink some more water, damn you. Time is a-wasting."

Stuart, talking with care, like a man whose stomach was tied together with string, said: "Tell us what's on your mind, Battles. And make it quick and simple."

That's exactly what Battles did, told his story plain, with no embroidery.

When he was finished, Durango said: "When is what's his name . . . Mad Dog . . . planning his attack?"

"During the first watch, at six bells."

"What the hell does that mean, Battles?" Stuart said, his anger, made worse by sickness, flaring. "One day on a boat and you're Davy Farragut? What's six bells in American time?"

"Eleven o'clock," Battles said. "Tonight."

"Couldn't you have said that in the first place?" Stuart said.

He rose slowly to his feet, banged his head against a low beam, and soundly cursed Battles, his seasickness, the Pacific Ocean, the treachery of the *Lila*'s crew, and his signing on with Warful in the first damn place.

"Now you've alarmed the whole ship. Can we keep the noise down?" Battles said. "We don't want Donovan to know we're onto him."

His tirade over, but his dander still up, Stuart rounded on Tidy, who still stood on the hatch ladder.

"You," he said, "give me back my iron."

Tidy smiled. "On that coil of rope at your feet, Lon, as ever was."

After he picked up his gun, Stuart passed Durango his revolver and, still surly, said: "The balance is all wrong with that piece."

"It suits me," Durango said.

"Then more fool you," Stuart said. "It'll get you killed one day."

Durango thumbed back the hammer of his Colt and pointed the gun at Stuart's belly. "You want to try out its balance today, Lon?"

"Enough!" Battles said, his own anger rising. "You'll have a bellyful of fighting tonight, all the fight you want. Now split ass up the ladder and rouse the rest of the men. Get them on their feet before you tell them what's happening. And for God's sake, keep your voices down."

"Do we get the men on deck?" Stuart said.

"No. For the time being I want them to act real sick," Battles said.

"They won't need to act," Stuart said. "They're already sick as pigs."

"What about Warful?" Durango said.

"I'll tell him," Battles said. "Whatever we do next is his call."

Battles rapped on the door of Warful's cabin.

"Who . . . is . . . it?" The man's voice was slow, measured, a tormented belly thinning his words.

"Matt Battles. I need you on deck. We've got trouble."

Warful groaned. "Give me a few minutes."

"I'll be waiting," Battles said.

When the marshal came on deck, the moon had dropped low enough to rest its chin on the mountains along the coast. The northern trade wind still gusted fair, but now it had a honed edge that made Battles shiver after the thick, stifling heat of the lower deck. A lantern on the quarterdeck cast orange light on Battles's hat and shoulders, and somewhere in the darkness he heard the mutter of men as the hands went about the mysterious duties of the night watches.

Warful stepped out from the captain's cabin, looked around, saw Battles, and strode toward him. The giant's normally yellow face had a queer greenish tinge, but the skin still stuck tight to the skull.

"Mr. Battles," he said, "this better be good. My lady wife is in considerable distress from the infernal movement of the ship and she needs my constant care and attention."

"It won't take long," Battles said. "Just listen to what I have to tell you."

Warful heard the story in silence, and only when the marshal stopped talking, did he say: "Treachery, by God! I suspected Mad Dog was a wrong-hearted scoundrel, and now I know for sure."

He peered at Battles through the waning moonlight. "How are the men?"

"In Stuart's words, 'sick as pigs.'"

The bad news hit Warful like a fist. Finally he said: "We could strike first, but not with sick men."

"Uh-huh, it could be a chancy thing," Battles allowed.

"How will they be by six bells tonight? I'll need fighting men, not invalids."

"I don't know. Better, I hope."

"Then we'll fight a defensive battle and save the ship."

The sinking moon had left the night to the stars, and the sky blazed from horizon to horizon. The wind talked in the rigging and the sea whispered along the *Lila*'s sides.

"Warful," Battles said, having long since decided that this man didn't merit a respectful "Mr.," "kill too many sailors and this boat will go around in circles until we all starve or run aground."

"I'm aware of that," Warful said. He seemed not

to notice the lack of an honorific or he didn't care. "Kill Mad Dog and the rest will buckle under. Once they see their captain laid out with coins on his eyes, the fight will go out of the dogs."

"I hope you're right," Battles said. "One thing we don't want to see is a deck littered with dead seamen."

Warful smiled. "Or gunfighters, Mr. Battles. Or gunfighters."

Chapter 26

A Dangerous Invitation

Mad Dog Donovan appeared on deck after breakfast and seemed friendly enough, though half a dozen tough sailors loitered close, keeping an eye on him.

Battles was on deck with Stuart, Durango, and several other gunmen who felt well enough to venture into the fresh air.

The *Lila*, starting to feel the effect of the south-blowing trade wind, heeled to starboard, but still managed to keep up a good clip, glassy seawater cascading over her fo'c'sle.

"How are you feeling, mates?" Donovan said, grinning. "Is the *Lila*'s humble fare agreeing with you? I like to see a cove eat as sails along o' me."

Nobody answered, but all stared blankly at the man.

Mad Dog rubbed his belly. "You take me, now. There's a man who loves his grub, you'll say. Aye, and you wouldn't be far wrong."

He picked between his upper teeth with a horny thumbnail.

"Fried salt pork is Mad Dog's meat, along o' eggs, runnylike, an' ship's biscuit, right tasty if you leave the weevils where they be."

Donovan's speech had the desired effect. A couple of gunmen, hands over their mouths, ran to the rail and retched.

Even Battles began to feel queasy.

"You think this sea is bad?" Donovan said. "Ha, we're a toy boat in a pond compared to where we're headed. Then where's worse, says you? Why, I says, it's the Horn, lads. Aye, in Drake's Passage I've seen waves as high as the top o' the mizzen, and them was the small ones. She'll pitch and roll, this one, and all the time many a lively sailorman with the sea's sickness will wish he was dead, even more than you lads are feeling now."

Donovan watched another gunman stagger to the rail, and, his mad eyes calculating, he said: "Why, I mind well the time off Tierra del Fuego—"

"Captain Donovan, don't you have duties that command your attention?" Battles said.

The marshal had his eye on Lon Stuart. The Texan would not be pushed, and Mad Dog with his talk of salt pork and high seas was dancing on his toes. Stuart's fingertips tapped the handle of his Colt, and the posture of his shoulders told Battles he was ready for the draw and shoot.

Maybe Mad Dog saw it too, because he broke into a smile and said: "There I go. As soon as I gets a-talkin' to shipmates, why, damn my eyes, I won't be silenced for man nor devil." He gave Battles a slight bow. "You're right, matey, I must be about my duties, as you were so kind to point out, like."

Donovan made to step away, but stopped and turned.

"Oh, I near forgot," he said. "I think you lads are gold dust, not a pushing bunch of lubbers at all. An' that's why tonight at six bells in the first watch I've ordered up a double tot of grog for all hands, and Fighting Tom Clancy from Dublin Town will play his fiddle. Now, then, me and the lads would admire if you'd join us."

Battles opened his mouth to speak, but Donovan held up a hand and said: "Well, says you, that's right handsome o' Cap'n Donovan and we'll gladly attend. But, says I, we're all shipmates here, so leave them guns behind. It's unfriendly, like, and a rum go to be sure."

Battles smiled. "And will your sailors have guns, Cap'n? Or cutlasses?"

"Bless you, sir, no," Donovan said. "Grog an' fiddlin' is what we're after." He turned to the sailors around him. "Is that not so, mates?"

The seamen nodded in agreement, and one hulking brute said: "Double grog was never ol' Poke's way, so all we want is to take pleasure in Mad Dog's generosity an' wet our pipes, like."

Another murmur of agreement rose from the sailors, and Battles said: "Then we'll attend and leave our weapons behind."

Donovan clapped his hands and beamed. "Didn't I tell you, lads? Gold dust. Lubbers to a man, mind, but gold dust just the same."

Stuart watched Mad Dog and his seamen go, then said to Battles: "Leave our guns behind? Are you out of your mind?"

"I don't want Donovan to feel that anything is amiss," the marshal said. "With so many men down, right now we're not in any shape for a fight. I hope to God that come six bells we are."

Chapter 27

Death of the Albatross

As the day twilighted into evening, the gunmen recovered enough to wash their filthy clothes in seawater and lie bare-chested on the deck.

The men were aware of Mad Dog's plans, but, at Matt Battles's insistence, they kept their guns below under guard.

Warful, older, still sick and confined to his cabin by his wife, was out of it for now, and Battles guessed he would take no part in the fight.

An hour into the first watch, the wind dropped and the *Lila*'s sails flapped like damp laundry on a clothesline. Mad Dog tacked the ship to the southwest, trying to catch the trade wind, but the *Lila* slowed to a stop and rolled at the mercy of the waves.

Under sail, a ship is a living thing that groans and creaks and talks to the wind and sea, but a stillness fell on the deck, and men were made uneasy by the ghostly silence.

Battles glanced at the lowering sun and wished for night.

"Watching it won't make it set any earlier, Battles," Lon Stuart said.

The marshal smiled. "I want the damned thing over with, I guess."

"The men will be ready."

"Remember, I want those swivel guns secured," Battles said.

"Tidy spoke to Ben Lane and Luke Anderson. They've used cannon before and they say they'll man the scatter guns."

"Then all we can do is wait for dark."

"You scared, Battles?" Stuart said.

To his surprise, the marshal had to think before answering.

"No," he said, "I don't think I am."

Stuart nodded. "You any idea how many kinds of hell a bunch of fast guns can unload on pilgrims crammed together on a deck like this?"

"Yeah, I have a good idea."

Battles was silent for a few moments, then said: "I'll tell you what I told Warful—we can't leave the deck littered with dead seamen. Do that and we'll have nobody left to sail the ship."

Stuart shrugged. "Hell, seamen, sailors, they'll have to take their chances like everyone else."

"Just don't kill them all," Battles said, "or this ship will become our floating coffin."

The night came cloudy, moonless, moody, the sullen sea flat as a billiard table.

For reasons known only to itself, an albatross rode air currents higher than the ship's masts and, like a gray ghost, kept pace with the drifting *Lila*.

After an hour, a sailor appeared on deck with a rifle and shot the bird, then watched it spiral into the sea.

Battles, who stood in the shadow of the starboard shrouds, heard Mad Dog's voice rise in an outraged scream.

"Damn you, Lem Samuels! By thunder, there's bad luck for all hands, an' no mistake." He wrenched the rifle from the seaman's hands. "Why did you shoot the bird?"

Samuels gave the slack-jawed grin of the mentally impaired.

"Fer sport, Cap'n," he said. "I wanted to make the bird to drop."

"It was an albatross, you idiot, a spirit bird," Donovan said. "You've brung us ill luck in full measure, by God."

"If our affair goes bad this night—" a seaman began, but Mad Dog hushed him with a foul oath.

"No more o' that, Bill," said he. "Our affair—I won't put a name to it—is not to be mentioned by you or me or anyone else until the business is over and done. Are ye catching my drift, Bill?"

"Aye, Cap'n, I am," the man called Bill said.

Mad Dog turned on Samuels again. "As for you, as now looks me atween the eyes as bold as brass like you reckon you're a gentleman in a cocked hat, I'll tickle your back with the cat come morning."

He grabbed the unfortunate Samuels by his shirtfront and pulled him close to his snarling face. "We'll see if thirty of the best cuts the sporting instincts out of ye, lay to that."

Battles heard a thud as Donovan pushed Samuels to the deck, and then there was silence.

At fifteen minutes before six bells, all the gunmen were up on their feet, though several of them were still queasy.

As a fiddler on the deck above scraped out "Paddy Doyle's Boots," then "Yankee Whalermen," Battles again pleaded with the gunmen to spare as many of the sailors as they could.

"Then tell them to spare us, if they could," Dee O'Day said. And the men laughed.

But Battles didn't join in the merriment. Stuart had been right. On the close confines of the deck, the enemy crowded together, a score of skilled gunfighters could, in a few seconds, do horrendous execution.

Somehow he had to keep the casualties among the seamen low.

And that meant killing their ringleader.

"Come on, you lads below, we're a-waiting for ye."

Mad Dog stood at the top of the ladder that led to the crew's quarters.

"We'll be right there," Battles said, lifting his Colt from Durango's waistband.

"Come friendly, like, ye understand?" Donovan said. "Just as though you was visiting kinfolk, which ye are, since we're all shipmates here an' mean you no harm."

Battles made no answer, and Mad Dog said: "Hurry now, mates, afore all the grog is drunk."

The man's feet thudded on the deck as he walked away.

"Everybody know what to do?" Battles said.

"Since Warful ain't here, you're the general, lawman," Stuart said. "Just don't mess it up."

"I'll do my best not to," Battles said. He looked around him in the guttering lamplight. "Lane, Anderson, I want you on deck first to secure the swivel guns."

Anderson, a hulking, menacing figure, spat and said: "You know how many times you've told me that?"

"Just making sure you don't forget."

"Well, now, that ain't likely, is it?"

"Right, then up on deck, you and Lane," Battles said.

He waited until the two gunmen mounted the ladder and disappeared into the darkness before saying to the others: "Let's go, and for pity's sake keep it quiet."

Chapter 28

The Fuse Is Lit

The gunmen immediately swarmed onto the quarterdeck and lined the rail, every man's gun up and ready. Anderson and Lane had already manned the swivel guns that were now pointed forward where the sailors were assembled.

Matt Battles had insisted on the lamps staying lit, so Mad Dog could see the force he faced and perhaps have second thoughts about taking over the ship. To his relief, Judah Rawlings, his face stiff as he looked straight ahead, was at the wheel.

The scramble onto the quarterdeck had been carried out so quickly, Donovan had no time to react.

But now, as six bells rang and the fiddler played "Poor Sally Sits A-Weeping," he left his assembled men and strode toward the quarterdeck, his face black with rage.

He turned his head as he walked and yelled: "You, Tom Clancy, belay that racket. It seems there are them here as don't want to hear it."

Mad Dog stopped and looked up at Battles.

"Now, what's the meaning of this?" he said. "Are ye refusing of my 'ospitality that you come at my poor sailormen, who never meant you no harm, with murderous revolvers in hand?"

"Tell your men to lay down their weapons, Donovan," Battles said. "Nobody need die here tonight."

"Ah, so that's the way of it," Mad Dog said. "No Cap'n if you please, just plain Donovan."

To prevent the decks running with the blood of skilled seamen, the fight had to come down to just him and Mad Dog, and Battles pushed hard.

"You're no captain, Donovan, just a half-hung rogue," he said. "And before we're done tonight I plan to finish the job the Dutch started."

"Damn your eyes, but that's harsh talk," Mad Dog said. "Have ye been a-turnin' your ear to sea stories?"

139

"Only one—the one that says you planned to cut the throats of these men here, turn the *Lila* about, and sell the gold in Mexico."

Mad Dog moved his head slowly, like a reptile, and his eyes moved to the man at the wheel.

"Judah Rawlings," he said, "you've been a-telling stories."

"Rawlings told me nothing that's not common knowledge on this ship," Battles said. He didn't want the helmsman to take any part of the blame for what was about to happen.

"You up there," Mad Dog said, "I'll go have what ye might call a consultation with my poor sailormen, and tell them how you've been listening to stories and are steering a course toward shooting and the bashing of heads."

"Then be quick about it, Donovan," Battles said. "I want this thing settled."

Stuart, his eyes like ice, heightened his sense of urgency.

"The hell with all this talk," the Texan said. "I'll gun the son of a bitch and be done."

"No, not yet," Battles said. "If you kill him now, we'll have a war on our hands."

"That's what we want, isn't it?" Stuart said.

Battles's irritation flared. "Damn it, for the hundredth time, we can't kill the sailors."

Stuart glanced at the silent rigging and listless sails.

140

"Hell, how hard can it be?" he said. "We can sail this tub."

Battles smiled. "Yeah, right onto the nearest rock."

Mad Dog, his head bent, had been in deep discussion with the crew.

He straightened and stepped toward the quarterdeck. This time the seamen, most armed with rifles, fanned out behind him.

Anderson and Lane tensed at the swivel guns.

The cannons were loaded with canister and could sweep the deck like a hailstorm. Few would still be standing when the smoke cleared.

"I've been a-talking to my lads, and here it is," Mad Dog said. "We want the gold, and we'll take it, but we've something to offer. And what might that be? says you. Well, says I, I'll say it plain, the only way this poor sailorman knows how."

"Let's hear it, Donovan," Battles said.

On either side of him the gunmen were ready, the sight of the seamen's rifles making them uneasy.

"I'll find a pleasant cove and drop all of ye off, safe and sound on a friendly shore, like," Donovan said. "Along o' that, you'll have one, no, two, kegs of gold. On that you have my affydavy, my word of honor."

Mad Dog raised his arms in an attitude of supplication. "There it is, all laid out for you.

Why, the cap'n can't say handsomer than that, says you. And it's right you'd be on that score, mates."

Battles took time to build and light a cigarette, the flaring match highlighting the flat planes of his face.

"Are you finished?" he said finally.

"Aye, and what's said to you is said to all. Refuse my offer and this deck will run red with blood."

Talking through a haze of blue smoke, Battles said: "And here are my terms—order your seamen to lay down their arms and return to their duties. Later you can discuss with Warful how the gold should be shared."

"Is that your last word?" Mad Dog said.

"Donovan, my talking is done."

"Then it's war atween us, matey," Mad Dog said. "An' many a lively lad a-standin' on yon quarterdeck will curse this day."

The fuse was lit. . . .

Appalled, Battles saw that both sides were ready to shoot it out.

He had to do something—fast!

Then Judah Rawlings left the wheel and whispered into Battles's ear . . . and showed him the way.

Chapter 29

A Clash of Steel

"Wait!" Matt Battles yelled.

He vaulted the quarterdeck rail and landed on his feet, a jarring leap for a man with thirty-six-year-old knees.

Biting back a painful reminder of his maturity, he held up a hand and yelled to Mad Dog: "Donovan, you run this ship by the Pirate Code. Under the code, I demand the right to challenge you for the captaincy of this vessel, as laid down by Edward Teach and . . . and . . ."

"Henry Morgan," Mad Dog said. "Damn your soul to the deepest sloughs of hell, I know the law."

"Then it's between you and me," Battles said. "Winner takes all."

"I'm a one-handed man, but I won't turn and show my stern to any man," Mad Dog said. "But I'm no fancy Texas draw fighter with a Colt's gun in my pants."

"Cap'n," a seaman said, "since you're the challenged party, the code says the choice of weapons is your'n."

"Says I, you're dead right, Sam, and so it does, wrote down in blood by old Blackbeard's own hand." Mad Dog looked across the deck at

Battles. "Do you give me the choice of weapons?"

"Choose any weapon you want, Donovan," Battles said, a sinking feeling in his gut.

Damn it, that was a really, really bad move.

And so it turned out.

Mad Dog's eyes glittered. "Bring me the cutlass bequeathed to me by my own sweet pa, as was hung in an iron cage from the Plymouth town gallows and left to dry in the sun. And, hear you, a pot o' grog as well."

A seaman offered Donovan the rum, but he said: "Set it on the port rail there, me lad." He grinned at Battles. "Afore that pot is emptied, I'll see the color of your guts."

A sailor gave the marshal a cutlass, a broad-bladed, heavy weapon with a curved iron hand guard.

But Mad Dog's sword looked as though it were crafted by a demon blacksmith in the Devil's forge.

The entire hand guard was covered by a grinning yellow skull, a silver coin set in the middle of its forehead.

Donovan raised the cutlass high and strutted around the deck like a gladiator in an arena.

"Lookee, lads," he said, "the skull of me own sweet pa that I paid ten silver shillings for in Plymouth Town after he died bad, and he's never let me down in a fight."

"He were a rum go, your pa, and afeard of no man," an older seaman said.

Donovan said: "Truer words was never spoke, Dan'l Clancy. I have the only piece of him that ain't roasting in hell and it's always guided my steel."

Lon Stuart stepped beside Battles.

"You ever used one of them swords before?" he said, nodding to the cutlass in Battles's hand.

The marshal, his eyes on the boasting, posturing Mad Dog, shook his head.

"Well, if he guts you like a hog, I'll gun the son of a bitch," Stuart said.

"Thanks," Battles said. "I appreciate your thoughtfulness."

"Don't mention it," Stuart said.

Mad Dog took a swig of rum, stepped out of his shoes, then walked into the middle of the deck, swinging his cutlass, grinning.

Immediately a sailor ran out with a bucket and sprinkled sand between him and Battles.

"When his blood starts a-gushin', I don't want ye to slip on the deck, Cap'n," he said.

Mad Dog nodded, but said nothing. All his attention was now focused on Battles.

The marshal stepped toward him, holding his cutlass low, the tip pointed upward.

Mad Dog feinted a thrust that Battles tried to defend, but, like the flickering tongue of a snake, the man's blade withdrew and then swung in an arc, the razor-sharp blade slicing into the right side of Battles's face.

Donovan stepped back, threw his sword point into the deck, where the blade stood swaying, and reached out his hand. A sailor gave him the grog pot and he drank deeply.

He looked across at Battles. "Ol' Cap'n Silas Higgs teached me that move," he said. "Did you enjoy it?"

A seaman laughed. "He was a devil, was ol' Silas."

"That he was," Mad Dog said. "An' right now him and my own sweet pa are watching us from hell, lay to that."

Battles tasted the blood in his mouth, and when he touched his cheek, his hand came away scarlet and wet.

Anger flared in him and he charged Donovan, his cutlass raised for a killing, downward slash.

Without seeming to hurry, Mad Dog passed his mug to a seaman, plucked up his sword, and parried Battles's blow, steel clashing against steel.

Again, Donovan recovered expertly and swung his cutlass in a flashing arc, the blade slamming into Battles's left side, cutting deep.

Gasping from shock and pain, Battles staggered a step back and dropped his guard.

This time Mad Dog went after him.

The man was a master swordsman. In his hand the cutlass's slow, clumsy blade was as quick and nimble as a rapier.

He pranced around on his bare feet like a dancer, and methodically cut Matt Battles to pieces. Donovan took his time, drawing out Battles's death, but the marshal soon looked like a man who'd fallen into a vat of crimson dye, blood streaming from cuts to his head, face, and upper body.

Finally Mad Dog stepped back, drained his grog to the last drop, and tossed the pewter pot away.

His sword grasped under his armpit, he wiped his mouth with the back of his hand. "Now I'll end it and put you out of your misery, matey," he said. "Says you, that's real civil of the cap'n, because I'm all cut to collops. Says I, well, I've had my fun and after I kill you I'll have another pot o' grog and drink it while you're feeding the sharks."

Mad Dog came at Battles again, crouched low, his lips drawn back in a feral snarl, the cutlass skull gleaming yellow in the lantern light.

Battles, down on one knee, had lost blood and he felt weak and nauseated. The cutlass in his hand was suddenly as heavy as an anvil and he staggered when he rose to again face a skilled enemy.

Mad Dog, sensing the kill, came at him slowly, and Battles heard the soft *swish . . . swish . . .* of his feet on the sand and the sound of the man's steady breathing.

Summoning all the strength that was left to him, Battles stepped forward and thrust for Donovan's throat. The man parried easily, contemptuously, then feinted a cut at Battles's left side. The marshal took a step to his right to avoid the blow—but fell into Mad Dog's trap.

The seaman swung his left arm, and the ivory-covered stump slammed like a club into Battles's head.

Battles took the terrific blow just above his right temple and, momentarily stunned, staggered back an ungainly step or two, then crashed onto his back.

Lon Stuart had to jump to the side to avoid Battles's falling body.

He looked down at the marshal and said: "You're done."

"The hell I am," Battles croaked, his ears ringing, the deck cartwheeling around him.

Mad Dog loomed into his line of vision and screamed in triumph. He drew back his sword, ready for the kill.

When Matt Battles was a boy, he and his friends had spent hours throwing their Barlow knives at trees. But unlike most of the others, he could never get his blade to stick. Usually it bounced off the trunk, to the jeers of his more skilled companions.

Therefore it was desperation and fear that forced him to throw the cutlass.

His right arm was down by his side, the sword in his hand. He swung fast and hard at Mad Dog, but instead of following through, he released the handle of the cutlass.

He was destined to miss, and the blade should've harmlessly crossed Donovan's body and clattered to the deck behind him.

But, as the cutlass left his hand, Battles's little finger snagged on the bottom of the iron guard, deflecting the blade just enough.

Such was the minuscule difference between life and death.

The cutlass flew straight with terrific velocity and buried itself to the hilt in Mad Dog's belly.

The man looked down at the sword sticking out of him, his face a mix of disbelief and horror. He took a step back, still staring at the sword, then another. Finally he fell on his back, his own weapon clanging onto the deck.

Battles was beyond rage, beyond reason, possessed by something primitive and mindlessly violent.

He staggered to his feet, stepped to Mad Dog, and pulled the sword from his belly.

He lurched toward the sailors, who drew back

149

from him, their wide eyes registering shock and fear.

"Damn you, damn you all," Battles screamed. "Are there any of you wants to challenge me?"

Battles waited, a glistening scarlet pillar with the eyes of a madman.

"Fight me, you bastards," he yelled. "You pack of craven bilge rats, fight me."

The sword was wrenched from Battles's hand.

"You've done enough fighting for one day, lawman," Stuart said. "It's over."

Battles opened his mouth to object, but the words faded in his throat.

Suddenly the deck rushed toward him . . . and he plunged headlong into darkness.

Chapter 30

A Ship of Ill Omen

The sound of birdsong or the face of a pretty woman on the pillow next to him is a pleasant way for a man to wake. But when Matt Battles opened his eyes only to look into the skull face of Hatfield Warful, the experience was far from pleasurable.

Behind Warful stood Lon Stuart and it was he who spoke first.

"You look like hell, lawman," he said.

Battles glanced around him. He lay on a bunk

in a small, narrow cabin with a low ceiling. The place was hot and stuffy and smelled of sweat.

"You're in Mad Dog's cabin," Stuart said. "He's got no use for it anymore."

"He's dead?" Battles said, surprised that his voice was a weak, dry croak.

"And buried," Stuart said. "We threw him and his pa, what's left of him, over the side."

Battles moved his eyes to Warful. "Where are we?"

"Off the coast of Peru, according to Judah Rawlings," Warful said.

"How . . . how long . . . ?"

"Five days," Stuart said. "For a while there we didn't think you were going to make it."

"You lost a lot of blood, you understand," Warful said. "Mad Dog just about cut you to ribbons."

"He's right about that, lawman," Stuart said. "You was never pretty before, but now you'll have scars all over your kisser."

"The ladies will love them," Warful said. "For some reason they do adore that kind of thing."

Battles felt the movement of the ship and, as though reading his mind, Warful said: "We've had a fair wind for the last four days. The *Lila* is the fastest bark on the seven seas in my opinion."

"How is the crew taking the death of Mad Dog?" Battles said.

Warful's face stiffened. "I appointed Rawlings as temporary captain, but he says the sailors are

151

still a bunch of mutinous dogs. That's why I took their weapons and have armed men on the deck at all times."

"Will they try to take over the ship again?" Battles said.

"Perhaps when we reach port, but not before," Warful said. "The heart went out of them when you killed Mad Dog, but perhaps they'll bide their time and wait until our guard is lowered."

The man grimaced, an expression that, for him, passed as a smile.

"You must get well, Mr. Battles," he said. "Great riches are waiting for all of us at the end of this voyage, and I want you to have your fair share. You surely deserve it."

After Warful and Stuart left, Judah Rawlings stepped inside bearing a small tray with a steaming bowl and a couple of ship's biscuits.

"How are you feeling, Matt?" he said. "Or should I say, Cap'n?"

Battles managed a smile. "I'm not the captain," he said. "You are."

"The seamen don't think that way. By the old pirate law you won the captaincy fair and square when you skewered Mad Dog."

"Then you'll be my assistant, Judah," Battles said.

"Beggin' your pardon, sir, that would be first mate, in seaman's terms, like."

"Then it is first mate you are."

He sniffed the bowl. "What the hell is that? It smells terrible."

"Portable soup, straight from the cask, for invalids as can't stomach regular ship's grub. An' it's the same recipe as laid down by Her Majesty's navy in the time of Nelson and used by seamen of every stripe since."

Battles was suspicious. "What's in it?"

"Why, bless you, sir, it's made from water, beef shinbone, bacon hock, anchovies, carrots, celery, and cayenne pepper."

"Then it will either cure me or kill me," Battles said.

"That it will, sir," Rawlings said.

After three days in his bunk, Battles had had enough. His face and sides were still heavily bandaged, but he felt stronger, despite Rawlings's portable soup.

According to the acting captain, the *Lila* was ten miles off the coast of Argentina and he said that, if the trade wind held, they should reach the Horn in another week.

"As for the Horn," Rawlings said, "well, no man can predict what will happen. We may get blown all the way back to San Francisco if there are gales in the Strait of Magellan and the williwaw winds are rising."

"What's that, a williwaw wind?" Battles said.

"It's a mighty storm wind that blows up without warning," Rawlings said. "Aye, and it's sent many a fine craft to the bottom in the blink of an eye and all her crew with her."

Rawlings winked. "Still, don't worry, Cap'n. We might have a clear passage. I say that even though the death of the albatross weighs heavy on me. It was bad luck to shoot the bird, lay to that."

After this melancholy intelligence, Battles was cheered by the sight of a beautiful steamship that overtook the *Lila* to starboard.

Warful and Judah Rawlings were less enchanted by the steamer when they stepped to the rail.

"What do you make of her, Mr. Rawlings?" Warful said.

"She's a steam frigate of thirty guns, beggin' your pardon, Mr. Warful, and she's flying the Argentine flag."

"Will she molest us?"

"Them Argentines don't trust the British or the Spanish, but we're flying the Stars and Stripes," Rawlings said. "The only thing is . . ."

"Is what?" Warful said, irritated.

"Her captain can see we're low in the water, and he'll know we're not carrying ballast in these seas." Rawlings shook his head. "I've heard o' cargoes being confy-scated by Argentines, but never paid them stories much mind. That is, until now."

Several officers on the frigate's deck studied the *Lila* with telescopes, but the ship made no attempt to sail closer.

"She hasn't beat to quarters," Rawlings said, "so she probably means us no harm."

"Perhaps she's afraid of us," Warful said.

"Dear heart, no," Rawlings said. "She could lie off a cable's length and in a trice cannon us into matchwood."

To Battles's relief, the frigate's stern dipped and she headed south at flank speed.

"I think our flag deterred her," Warful said. He stared hard at Rawlings. "Remember, Captain, this ship carries a cargo much more precious than gold—my lady wife."

Rawlings knuckled his forehead. "I'll remember your missus, bless her heart."

After Warful stepped away, Rawlings looked at Battles and said: "As though I could forget her, the way she stinks up the whole damned ship."

"Will we see that frigate again?" Battles asked.

"Ah," Rawlings said. "You feel it, then."

"Feel what?"

"That she's a ship of ill omen."

Battles nodded. "Yeah, I feel it."

Chapter 31

The Rocket's Red Glare

"I don't like a fog," Judah Rawlings said. "There are sea creatures come out in a fog and the damned souls of old pirates, and they grabs poor sailormen a-screaming off the deck."

"I can't see a damn thing," Battles said. "And the wind has dropped to a whisper."

Rawlings was taking a turn at the wheel, since he was the best helmsman on board and the fear of running aground on a lee shore troubled the sailors.

"There's breeze enough to see us through, lay to that," Rawlings said. "But there's evil in the fog, damn it to hell."

The mist curled around the masts and lay so thick on the deck that the seamen on watch moved around like gray ghosts. The shrouded sea was silent, unmoving, so calm that the *Lila* could have been shored up in dry dock.

Warful and the gunmen were below, not liking the fog, yet horrifyingly captivated by the tales of straight-faced sailors who related their encounters with sea serpents and the perils of the southern latitudes off the African coast where the Dutchman and his doomed crew lured poor mariners to their destruction.

Rawlings raised his nose, as though smelling the wind, but when he turned his head to Battles he said: "Hear that?"

"Hear what?"

"Listen."

Battles, all his senses alert, listened into the somber day.

"I don't hear anything," he said finally.

"It's back," Rawlings said. "The frigate we met yesterday is out there somewhere."

Again Battles listened and this time he heard it, the faint *chunk . . . chunk . . . chunk . . .* of a slow-turning screw off their starboard bow.

"Damn it, she's searching for us," he said.

Rawlings nodded. "She's a pirate, lay to that, but she'll do it nice and legal like. Her captain can claim the right of maritime law to stop and search any ship within his nation's territorial waters."

"Are we in their territorial waters?" Battles said.

"No, but an Argentine man-o'-war won't quibble about feet and inches when there's booty to be had."

Rawlings ordered quiet on deck and the *Lila* glided silently through the fog.

When he rejoined Battles at the rail, the marshal said: "I should get Warful and his men on deck. The Argentines may try to board us."

"Belay that," Rawlings said. "One o' them

Texans could take it into his head to do some shooting and draw the frigate right on top of us. No, for now we stay as quiet as a mouse and pray the cat passes us by."

The cat did not pass by.

After a few minutes of tense waiting, Battles heard the frigate's screw slow and then stop. An eerie silence fell over the sea, made even more unsettling by the fog that settled over and around the *Lila* like a burial sheet.

"She's listening for us," Rawlings whispered, touching his tongue to his dry top lip. "Stalking us, damn her."

Suddenly the man's weather-beaten face was stained scarlet and his eyes widened with shock.

The red halo of the flare hung in the sky for what seemed an eternity. Like clouds at sunset, crimson light tinted the gray billows of the fog and for a few seconds a patch of sea near the *Lila* rippled like molten iron.

The flare dropped, trailed sparks, then died.

A moment later a cannon boomed and a shell roared over the *Lila* at mast height. A few seconds passed, and then another fell somewhere ahead of the ship, its explosion lost in the fog.

"She's firing blind," Battles said to Rawlings. "Hoping we'll react."

Predictably, the gunmen reacted to the sound of firing.

Led by Lon Stuart, they tumbled onto the deck, all of them with guns drawn.

Stuart sought Battles in the fog, found him, and loudly demanded to know what the hell was going on.

Battles hushed the man into silence and said: "The frigate is back looking for us."

"Seems like they found us," Stuart said.

"They're firing probing shots," Battles said. He looked beyond Stuart to the other gunmen emerging from the mist. "You men keep quiet," he said. "The Argentine doesn't know where we're at."

That proved to be the case.

After a couple of other probing shots that came nowhere near the *Lila,* the frigate started her engines and the sound of her screws faded into silence as she headed back north.

When he was sure the ship was gone, Stuart said to Battles: "It dawned on me there that a six-gun ain't much use against a steam frigate."

"We were lucky," Battles said. "The fog saved us, or she'd have boarded us for sure."

"We've got to come back this way, laden with gold and treasure, if Mr. Warful is tellin' it right," Rawlings said. "And she'll be looking for us, lay to that."

Battles smiled. "I'm not going to build houses

on a bridge I haven't crossed yet. I'll worry about the frigate when the time comes."

"Oh yeah?" Stuart said. "Well, in the meantime I'm sure you won't mind if I do the worrying for both of us."

Chapter 32

At the Slave Port

Eight days after her brush with the frigate, the *Lila* rounded the Horn, sailing through the most unforgiving waters in the world.

But the dire warnings from the sailors about screeching winds and mountainous waves never came to pass.

Instead, though the sky was overcast, the sea was strangely, glassily calm, the air so clear the Horn was visible off the ship's port side.

The *Lila* was sluggish, her sails flapping for lack of a breeze, and Rawlings ordered out the jolly boats and kept his eye on the weather as sturdy members of the crew attempted to tow her into a trade wind.

Two days later they were still hard off the Horn.

Warful was beside himself with anxiety. He constantly berated Rawlings for the lack of wind and hinted darkly that if his lady wife grew much sicker, the captain would pay with his life.

The gunmen were also irritable, and heartily

sick of their salt-beef-and-biscuit diet. Dee O'Day, drunk on rum and boredom, pulled a gun on Durango, and only the fast action of Battles grabbing his wrist prevented a killing.

Cape Horn does bad things to a man's mind. The seas around the southern tip of South America are menacing, unpredictable, and he constantly feels uneasy, as if he's sharing a cave with a hungry grizzly that's just wakened from winter hibernation.

But the storms didn't pounce and on the third day the *Lila* picked up a trade wind. She rounded the Horn without difficulty and charted a heading northeast in the direction of the West African coast.

Backed by a fair wind and fine weather in the South Atlantic, the ship made good speed, and after forty-three days at sea, the *Lila* dropped anchor off the port of Eugene de Montijo.

"It's a sight to see, is it not, Mr. Battles?" Warful said as he and his hired gunmen crowded the ship's rail for their first glimpse of the bustling port.

The cuts on the marshal's face and body had healed into scars. If he hadn't been a homely man to begin with, his good looks would've been ruined.

"It's a busy place," he said.

The harbor was crowded with ships of all kinds, from sleek schooners to the wide-beamed, oceangoing dhows of Arab slave traders.

Warful looked around him and spoke to his gunmen. "Look beyond the town to the hill, gentlemen," he said. "The large marble edifice you see is the palace of His Majesty King Brukwe. The red and green flag is the monarch's personal standard."

"An' that's where the treasure is, huh?" Dee O'Day said.

"Indeed it is, Mr. O'Day," Warful said. "And very soon now it will all be ours."

"When are we going ashore, boss?" Luke Anderson said. "I need a woman real bad."

"There's plenty of doves in Eugene," Judah Rawlings said. "A man can get his barnacles scraped any time he feels like it."

"You'll be ashore soon, Mr. Anderson," Warful said. "But first I want to reconnoiter, get the lay of the land, like, and find out where the rich Jews live."

"I just want the lay," Anderson said. "The hell with the land."

This last raised a laugh among the gunmen and the few listening sailors, but it was cut short when a seaman on the quarterdeck yelled: "Jolly boat coming out."

The boat, rowed by two husky natives, bumped alongside the *Lila*, and a small, fat, and perspiring white man scrambled up the boarding ladder with surprising agility.

· · ·

After looking around for a few moments, the little man said: "Is Captain Yates available?"

Warful stepped in front of the visitor, two feet taller and intimidating.

"Captain Yates is deceased," he said. "I am Hatfield Warful."

The small man wore a white suit, much crumpled, and yellow arcs of sweat stained his coat at the armpits. He wore a dirty white shirt and a narrow, red and green tie.

"I'm sorry to hear that the captain's dead," he said. "How did he die?"

"Suddenly," Warful said.

"Then I will address you, Mr. Warful." He wiped sweat from his face with a huge handkerchief, returned it to his pocket, and said: "My name is Marcel Toucey, late of Marseilles Town, and I am—or I was—Captain Yates's agent in Eugene de Montijo. I trust the relationship I had with him will continue with you."

Warful accepted that with a slight bow. "Please go on," he said.

"Well, as to the Afrikaner mercenaries," Toucey said, "they won't be coming."

If Warful was disappointed, he didn't let it show.

"Why not?" he said.

"The British anticipate more trouble with the

163

Boers and are clamping down on them hard. They won't allow five hundred Boer cavalry to leave South Africa, or even stand by and let that many fighting men assemble in one place."

Toucey looked up at Warful and puffed out his plump cheeks.

"A glass of rum would not go amiss, Mr. Warful," he said.

"Of course." Warful looked at Rawlings. "A glass of rum for Mr. Toucey, Captain."

Rawlings gave the Frenchman his rum and after taking a deep swig, Toucey said: "There's talk of the British building what London calls 'concentration camps' for the wives and children of the Boers. The plan is that the Boer men won't be so eager to fight when they know their families are on starvation rations behind guard towers and barbed wire." He shrugged. "But, of course, they will fight."

For some reason Warful was intrigued. "What a singularly excellent idea." He held his chin, musing. "Concentration camps could be the answer to the Jewish problem."

Toucey was puzzled. "What Jewish problem?"

Warful shook his head. "No matter. I'll discuss it with you later."

The giant stepped to the rail and studied the palace through his telescope. He turned his head and said: "Mr. Toucey, can I take the palace with my gunfighters?"

The Frenchman stepped beside him. "How many do you have?"

"These you see around you."

"You don't have enough."

"Then I can use the crew of this vessel."

"You still won't have enough. The king's palace is well guarded and his troops have machine guns and artillery."

"Can I hire mercenaries in the town?" Warful said.

Toucey shook his head. "No. The only fighting men in Eugene de Montijo wear the uniform of King Brukwe."

Warful sighed. "Mr. Toucey, your bad news and pessimism have quite destroyed the tranquility of the morning." He advanced on the Frenchman, who suddenly seemed frightened. "You will accompany me on my reconnoiter of the town and point out the houses of the Jews." His skeletal face broke into a smile. "My lady wife has her heart set on a Jewish wedding ring."

"Plenty of wedding rings in the bazaars," Toucey said.

"Yes, but those won't do. My wife wishes one taken from the severed finger of a Jewess."

Matt Battles watched the Frenchman's face, and his look of horror told him that the little man realized what he himself already knew—that Warful was stark, raving mad . . .

And therefore dangerous beyond measure.

Chapter 33

The Iron Handmaidens

Built on a narrow strip of land, Eugene de Montijo was a crowded, noisy town. The crooked, teetering wooden houses, some as high as four stories, looked like dwellings from a fairy tale by the brothers Grimm, and rubbed shoulders with raucous taverns and exotic stores with red or yellow or blue awnings. Set among this clamoring cacophony of color and sound were warehouses with crowded slave pens attached, guarded by bearded Arabs shouldering French-made Gras rifles, scimitars hanging from their waists.

Even this early in the morning, the port's only street was crowded and Matt Battles was jostled by drunk sailors of a dozen nationalities, swarthy Arab traders and slavers, stiff-collared Englishmen sweating in broadcloth, quick, excitable Frenchmen, stately natives wearing only loincloths, Italians, Germans, Russians, and a few Indians, all talking at the top of their voices, a roaring, bellowing, deafening babel of languages and accents.

The hot air smelled of packed humanity, overlaid with the more languid scents of spices, rum, tobacco, and the blooming moringa trees.

Through this milling maelstrom Matt Battles, Durango, and Warful walked unnoticed, as though men in high-heeled boots and wide-brimmed hats were an everyday sight.

At Warful's insistence, both Battles and Durango were without their guns, this being only a reconnaissance and not, as he put it, "an armed invasion."

Marcel Toucey, constantly wiping his face with his handkerchief, pointed out the sights as they walked along the narrow street, including a tavern that he claimed had been built by a famous Barbary pirate, the Dutchman Jan Janszoon.

Gradually the buildings grew fewer and Toucey led Battles and the others into an area where bazaars selling everything from black female slaves to Chinese porcelain lined both sides of the street.

Indian and Arab vendors called out to them as they passed, promising unheard-of bargains, then cursed at them in languages they didn't understand as they walked past.

"Where is the Jewish quarter?" Warful asked Toucey.

The Frenchman shrugged. "All around you."

Warful nodded. "Then it will make it a little harder to roust them out, but I'll do it once I'm king."

Toucey said nothing, but his face was troubled.

"How much treasure does King what's-his-name have squirreled away?" Battles asked.

"A great deal, I should imagine, Mr. Battles," Toucey said. "His family has ruled Eugene de Montijo for two hundred years, and he takes a cut from every business in the port."

Warful smiled. "What happens if someone refuses to pay?"

"You'll see what happens very soon," Toucey said.

After the bazaars petered out, the road rose in a gradual slope and wound through a grove of acacia trees that threw a dappled shade. The trees gave way to an open, grassy area where insects chirped and the full heat of the sun hammered mercilessly.

King Brukwe's palace stood at the top of the rise, a sprawling stucco brick mansion built in the French colonial style.

Trimmed hedges lined the curved driveway in front of the house, and the grounds were beautifully landscaped, using native plants and flowers. Birds sang and added to the serenity of the palace and grounds.

Therefore, the sight of rotting bodies in iron cages suspended from the roof and the female soldiers standing guard at the arched entrance was all the more jarring.

"That's what happens to people who don't pay

the king's taxes, Mr. Warful," Toucey said. "They're strung up in a cage and left to dry in the sun."

The two guards at the arch were joined by two more, and all four women looked at the approaching men with open suspicion and hostility.

Apart from an ammunition bandoleer across their chests, the guards were bare-breasted. Each wore a beaded headband and leather kilts and sandals and they carried British rifles.

Battles figured the women were young, no more than twenty, their breasts, which had obviously never suckled a child, high and firm.

"This is as far as we go," Toucey said. "Those Amazons are King Brukwe's Iron Handmaidens and they'll shoot first and ask questions later."

Battles looked to the north where army tents were pitched in orderly rows on flat, treeless ground, the French tricolor flapping above the largest.

"Who are they?" he asked Toucey.

"A regiment of French infantry," the man answered. "The kingdom's border with French West Africa is only half a mile away at this point."

Warful seemed troubled. "Why are they there, right on our doorstep?"

Toucey shrugged, a habit of his. "A show of

169

strength, aimed at intimidating King Brukwe. Every so often the French will move troops to the border, to keep the peace and suppress the slave trade, they say. The real reason is to make sure Paris gets its fair share of the kingdom's spoils."

"When I attack the palace, will the French intervene?" Warful said.

"I don't know," Toucey said. "It all depends on the mind of the commander of the regiment down there. There have been Arab trader tax revolts against King Brukwe in the past, almost bloodless certainly, but still, the French were content to stand aside. They may do it again."

"Where are the cannons and the Gatling guns?" Battles said.

The Frenchman smiled again. "I don't know that either, but I suspect the Iron Handmaidens can roll them out very quickly."

Warful turned to Durango. "We will land the men today, but my lady wife will stay on board until we take the palace." He smiled. "If you find a married Jewess, bring her to me."

Now he looked at Toucey. "Where is the palace garrison?"

"You can't see it from here, but they have a permanent barracks on the other side of the hill."

Warful thought about that. "I could attack there first and scatter them."

"There are two hundred of them," Battles said, stunned at the man's arrogance.

"They're blacks," Warful said. "They won't stand against white men."

Even Durango, not the most intelligent of men, looked doubtful when he heard that statement.

And Toucey said: "King Brukwe's soldiers are Fulani, great warriors. They'll stand their ground and fight."

"That, my dear Toucey, remains to be seen," Warful said. "What a frightened little man you are, to be sure."

"Mr. Warful," the Frenchman said, battling to keep his voice calm, "the Masai are mighty warriors, but they step around the Fulani. Even the Zulus, bravest of all, have never tangled with that tribe. The Fulani were nomads who converted to Islam centuries ago, and are so light-skinned other Africans refer to them as 'the white people.' "

Toucey shook his head. "They make unreliable friends and bad enemies."

"I have a score of my country's top gunfighters with me," Warful said. "We'll kill a hundred of them and scatter the rest."

"Is that your plan?" Toucey said. "You will not be dissuaded from your folly?"

"Folly?" Warful said, looking down his nose at the little Frenchman. "Perhaps it seems that way to lesser men, but to me it will be the realization of my destiny."

Toucey wiped his sweating face. "Then I wish

to have no more to do with you or your suicidal plan," Toucey said. "Of course, I still expect my promised share from the gold ship, and I want it soon. My agents will be in touch." He lifted his hat. "Now I wash my hands of you. Good day to you, sir."

Warful watched the man go, then turned to Durango. "I'll see that little man in hell before I'd give him a share of the *Lila*'s gold. Make sure that the nervous Mr. Toucey doesn't live out the day."

The gunman nodded. "I'll attend to it."

"I know you will," Warful said. "You're my good right hand that smites my enemies."

Chapter 34

At the Admiral Duperre

After Warful left in the *Lila*'s jolly boat, Battles and Durango hung around the dock and watched an Arab slave trader load chained slaves into the hold of a wide-beamed dhow.

A sailor with an English accent stopped beside them, watched the scene, then said: "Those poor blighters are bound for the Brazil rubber plantations. They'll all be dead in a year."

"Hard work, huh?" Durango said, only half interested.

The seaman nodded. "Hard work and starvation rations take their toll. But they mostly die of malaria or dengue fever. Yellow fever too, poor, doomed bastards."

The sailor seemed inclined to be sociable, so Battles said: "This is our first time in port. When will we catch sight of King Brukwe?"

"You won't. They say he's so fat he can't leave the palace. I heard he needs a winch to lower him on top of his harem women, and he's suffocated a few."

Suddenly Durango was interested. "How many women does he have?"

"The number is kept at fifty," the sailor said. "The king calls them his Iron Handmaidens, and they're his bodyguard as well as his wives."

The seaman inched closer. "Keep away from them women, mate. If they take a dislike to you, they'll cut your balls off and then impale what's left of you, ram a stake up your arse, you can lay to that."

He looked around him, then pushed his face even closer to Durango. "The very thing happened to a mate of mine, young Charlie Spooner off the old *City of Exeter* schooner. The poor lad tried to rape one o' them women and they impaled him. Charlie screamed on the stake for two days and on the third he couldn't scream no more. He died the day after that, a-thanking God for his deliverance."

"Good women to stay away from," Battles said.

The sailor's face was suddenly serious. "Aye, stay away from them women, says I. And listen, don't go near the palace, ever. Bad things happen to them as wander up the hill."

The man's face cleared and he smiled. "The good news is that there's plenty of willin' women in town who'll let you haul your hawser. Says I, there's no need to go after them Iron Handmaidens like poor Charlie Spooner an' get your balls cut off."

The sailor knuckled his forehead. "Well, good day to ye, gentlemen. All this woman talk has me thinking that it's time to find a tavern an' a willin' wench."

He stepped away with a rolling gait, as though he were walking a storm deck, then turned and said: "Mind what I told ye, now. Stay away from the palace. It's no place for a Christian man."

The crew ferried ashore in the jolly boats and Warful warned them to assemble on the dock at dusk for the return.

After the whooping gunmen dispersed into the town in search of rum and women, only Battles and Durango remained on the dock.

Warful stared at the gunman, then took a Colt from his waistband and passed it to him. "You have a job to do, Durango," he said.

The gunman nodded. "I'll find him."

"And when you do?"

"The moon won't shine on the Frenchman's fat ass tonight."

Warful's skull face stretched in a smile. "Then go do it."

After Durango left, Battles said: "What about me, Warful? You want me to kill somebody as well?"

The smile didn't leave Warful's face. "Sometimes you have a crude way of putting things, Mr. Battles. No, I don't want you to kill anyone, at least not for now."

Warful's eyes wandered beyond the dock to the sea.

"Ah," he said, pointing, "look yonder, Mr. Battles. Those dark triangles you see cutting through the water are sharks."

"I've heard of them, never seen one, though," Battles said.

"I saw a few in the Pacific," Warful said, "but they didn't come anywhere near the ship."

He shaded his eyes with a hand. "They're hunting close. It must be the time of year when fish shoal in these waters."

Warful took his eyes from the sea and said: "A glass of rum with you, Mr. Battles?"

The marshal nodded. "I could use one."

"Then let's find a reputable tavern, if such exists in this town."

The *Admiral Duperre* faced the docks and was frequented by clients of the better sort, mostly

175

ships' officers and local businessmen. A few pretty African women in low-cut buba blouses and tight, wrapped skirts, sat at the bar and showed off their charms, but the customers ignored them, or at least pretended they did.

The rum, served in crystal, was Jamaican and of good quality. Battles built a cigarette and for the first time that day began to relax. Only the ominous presence of Hatfield Warful prevented him from fully enjoying the exotic sights, smells, and sounds of his surroundings.

As it happened, Battles's pleasure was short-lived.

There was a sudden commotion in the street and men's voices were raised in anger. A rifle shot racketed, then another.

Dee O'Day backed through the tavern's open door, his right hand clawing for a gun that wasn't there.

His face wild, he looked around him, and saw Warful and Battles.

"What's amiss, Mr. O'Day?" Warful asked, rising to his feet.

It took O'Day a few moments of mouth movements, his throat bobbing, before he could answer.

"Luke Anderson killed a woman. He's been arrested and they're trying to round up everybody who was with him." O'Day, a frightened man, stepped to Warful. "That includes me," he said.

Chapter 35

Murder and Hostages

Warful jumped to his feet, his face moving.

"Damn you, O'Day," he said, forgetting the niceties. "What the hell happened?"

O'Day tried to answer, but the words jammed in his throat. Warful gave him his glass of rum.

"Drink this, then tell me," he said.

O'Day downed the rum in a gulp, then rubbed a nervous hand across his mouth before speaking.

"We was at a saloon just around the corner," he said. "Luke was real horny and soon found himself a dove. She took him upstairs and time passed. Then we heard screams. Next thing we know, another dove with blood on her hands runs into the street and hollers for help."

"Where is Anderson now?" Warful said.

"The soldiers took him."

"Women soldiers?" Battles asked.

"No, they were men, black men, or almost black. And now they're looking for me, damn them, even though I had nothing to do with the murder."

O'Day flared his anger at Warful. "And I don't have a gun. You told us to leave them on the damned boat."

Warful thought for a moment, then said: "Get down to the dock. Wait for me there."

But before O'Day could move, three soldiers burst into the tavern, a young woman with bloodstained hands in tow. She spotted O'Day immediately, pointed at him, and screamed something in a language Battles didn't understand.

The soldiers, dressed in the blue coats and red breeches of regular French infantry, surrounded O'Day with fixed bayonets and motioned him toward the street.

"Damned if I do!" O'Day yelled.

He ran at the nearest soldier, brushed his rifle aside, and made a dash for the door.

He almost got there.

Just as O'Day was about to run into the street, a soldier fired his Gras into the gunman's back. O'Day threw up his arms, staggered a step, and crashed onto his face. He groaned once, then lay still.

Now the rifles swung on Battles and Warful.

"Don't move," Battles said to Warful. "Don't even blink."

A few tense moments slid past; then the soldiers put up their rifles, grabbed O'Day by the arms, and pulled him away.

The smoke lingered in the closeness of the tavern, and the echoes of the gunshot rang in Battles's ears. He sat at the table and, his voice unsteady, said: "Damn, I need this drink."

The gunmen, most of them drunk, were at the dock by dusk. All but Durango, who had other business at hand.

By now the talk of Anderson's arrest and O'Day's death was all over town, and several of the gunmen, conspicuous in their boots and hats, had been roughed up by roaming gangs of irate citizens.

Lon Stuart spoke for the rest when he said: "I say we go back to the ship, get our guns, and come back and hooraw this damn town."

The other gunmen muttered or cursed their agreement, but Warful said: "That won't bring O'Day back or release Anderson from custody."

"Then what do we do?" Stuart said.

"Hostages," Warful said. "We'll exchange them for Mr. Anderson."

"Then let's get our guns," Stuart said.

"We don't need guns," Warful said. "Not for Jews."

"Where the hell do we find them?" Stuart said.

Warful turned and looked at Battles. "That tavern we were enjoying before the unpleasant incident with Mr. O'Day, did you notice anything?"

"The women at the bar," Battles said.

"There were elderly Semites there, at a table," Warful said. "They were drinking coffee while they argued interminably about something. I have a feeling they might still be there."

Before Battles had a chance to say anything, Warful turned away from him and said to his gunmen: "Mr. Stuart, you and five others come with me and Mr. Battles. The rest of you into the jolly boats and await our return."

He smiled. "It is said that King Brukwe loves his Jews. Let's see if he loves them well enough to release Luke Anderson."

Battles said: "If Anderson did kill a woman, he should stand trial for his crime here in Eugene de Montijo."

"There speaks the lawman," Stuart said. "Battles, you may have turned outlaw, but you're still wearing a star."

"I don't believe Mr. Anderson could get a fair trial in this town," Warful said. "But if it assuages your conscience any, Mr. Battles, when I sit on the throne with my lady wife as queen at my side, I will judge Mr. Anderson fairly and justly."

Warful turned his back on Battles, making it clear that he was no longer interested in anything he had to say.

Instead, to Stuart, he said: "Come, let's go Jew-hunting."

Chapter 36

Warful Pens a Letter

There was no question of Warful letting Matt Battles out of his sight, and he insisted that the marshal accompany him to the tavern.

The four old men, white-bearded and dressed in somber black, still sat at the table. The oldest had a Hebrew Bible open in front of him and was arguing vehemently about something when Warful, accompanied by Battles and six gunmen, stepped into the tavern.

Warful walked through the crowd and stopped at the table, looking down from his great height at the four men.

"Do any of you speak English?" he said.

It was the oldest graybeard who answered, his expression wary. "Yes, I speak English. What can I do for you?"

Warful lied smoothly. "There's a Jewish man at the dock who seems to be sick and in great distress, but he can't speak English. I wonder if you can come talk to him."

The old man closed his Bible and rose to his feet. "Of course I will," he said.

"This way," Warful said, bowing slightly, his arm extended toward the door.

The three other oldsters also rose and followed,

still arguing with one another, their hands expressing what their tongues could not.

Battles had stood by long enough.

He moved toward the door and tried to stop Warful. But Stuart and a couple of other gunmen intercepted him and jostled him back.

As Warful followed the old men out the door, Battles yelled: "Wait! Stop!"

He tried to break free of Stuart and the others, but something hard hit him on the back of his head and he collapsed in a heap on the floor.

Matt Battles woke to a splitting headache and a rage with the fuse lit.

He touched the back of his head, felt a lump, and reckoned he'd been hit with a bottle, probably swung by Lon Stuart, damn him.

Battles looked around him. He was surrounded by gloom but saw enough. He was on the ship, somewhere forward, in a small closet-sized room that contained nothing but a life belt and the rats that scuttled in the corners.

Later, looking back on it, he couldn't tell how long he'd been there when the door opened, allowing a shaft of thin light to enter.

"On your feet, Matt," Durango said. "The boss wants to talk with you."

"What about?"

"I guess he'll tell you his own self what about."

Battles smiled. "Durango, I'm so looking forward to the day I kill you."

The breed laughed. "You ain't got the speed nor the sand, Matt. You know it and I know it."

The closet wasn't high enough for a tall man to stand, and Battles was forced to crouch as he stepped through the doorway onto the deck.

It was morning and sand blowing off the Sahara painted the sky yellow, streaked with bands of jade and rust red.

Battles saw that Judah Rawlings had conned the *Lila* closer to land and she was now anchored only a pistol-shot distance from the dock.

Warful was on the quarterdeck, talking with Rawlings, and when he saw Battles he beckoned to him.

"This way, Mr. Battles, if you please," he said.

"Go to hell," Battles said, loud enough.

Warful merely smiled. "Then I take it you don't wish to go ashore and attempt to save your Jewish friends?" he said.

The man had dangled a baited hook and Battles took it.

"What I have here in my hand is a letter of marque, demanding that the authorities in Eugene de Montijo return what is mine, namely my hired man, Mr. Luke Anderson," Warful said.

He smiled, the early sun casting shadows in the

hollows of his eyes and cheeks, making his face more skull-like than ever.

"Since King Brukwe is the only authority in the city, you will hand the letter directly to him."

"And if I don't?" Battles said.

"Ah, and if you don't? Then I will send someone else. As is explained in the letter, if my demand is not met by noon, I will hang the Jew Jacob Bensoussan in full sight of the town. If there is any further delay, I will hang the other three two hours apart."

Warful stared out to sea, as though the matter was of complete indifference to him.

"Needless to say, Mr. Battles, if you do not deliver my letter, you will be complicit in the deaths of four Jews, including the respected rabbi, the said Jacob Bensoussan."

He again turned his attention to Battles. "Do I make myself perfectly clear?"

"Perfectly," Battles said. Then, his anger rising, he said: "Warful, Dee O'Day is already dead and by this time Luke Anderson probably wishes he was."

He was aware that Rawlings and a couple of other seamen were listening attentively.

"You'll lead everyone, your pack of outlaws and the crew of this ship, to their deaths chasing a madman's dream. Saddle up and ride on out of here while you still can."

Warful smiled. "All great men have a streak of

madness and I am no exception. But I will be king of Eugene de Montijo, never fear."

"Damn it," Battles said, "you don't have enough gunmen to take this city."

"No, I don't. I see that now. But the French have troops, and once they realize that I'm a very superior type of human being, they will take Eugene de Montijo for me and my lady wife."

Battles opened his mouth to speak, but Warful cut him off.

"This grows tiresome," he said. "Will you take the letter of marque or not? Must I send Durango in your stead? Mind you, he did not find Marcel Toucey, so he has already failed me once." Warful's grin was frightful. "Perhaps it's no matter. I admit that my lady wife hopes your mission will fail. She says she's eagerly looking forward to seeing Jews dance in the air."

"I'll take it, damn you," Battles said.

But he felt hope drain out of him like water from a holed bucket.

Now clutching the sealed letter in his hand, he realized he was as doomed as the rest.

Chapter 37

The Iron Cage

If Warful thought it strange that Judah Rawlings insisted on accompanying Battles, he didn't let it show and made no objection, saying only: "You can act as a courier, Captain, and let me know what's happening ashore."

As Battles left the ship, Lon Stuart stood by the rail and wished him luck.

Now that the Texan's anger over O'Day's death and Anderson's arrest had cooled, he seemed oddly subdued, as did several of the other gunmen.

King Brukwe's soldiers had acted ruthlessly and efficiently after the murder of the dove, and seemed well enough trained that they wouldn't, as Warful had claimed, cut and run at the first sound of shots fired in anger.

Battles smiled as he stepped down the ladder into the jolly boat.

Maybe the gunmen had begun to realize that the king's treasure would be harder to take then they'd been led to believe.

The marshal's smile slipped when he remembered that he'd have to get past the Iron Handmaidens, who were said to be even more ruthless than the soldiers.

No matter how he looked at it, delivering Warful's letter wasn't going to be easy.

"Delivering that letter ain't going to be easy, Matt," Judah Rawlings said as he rowed the boat toward the dock.

"Seems like," Battles said, pretending a confidence he didn't feel.

"How you going to get past them females?"

"I don't know."

The oars creaked in the locks and the ropy muscles of Rawlings's arms bunched as he battled an outgoing tide.

"You reckon Warful will really hang them old men?" he said.

"He'll hang them and enjoy doing it."

"I can't lay athwart that myself," Rawlings said. "I didn't know the Anderson cove personal-like, but from all I've heard he ain't a man worth saving."

"He isn't," Battles said, his eyes on the deck of the *Lila* where Warful had a telescope to his eye, watching the jolly boat's progress.

"Then hanging four old men to save his hide don't make sense, to me and to nobody else, an' that goes for my crew."

"It does to Warful. He'll hang them because he hates Jews."

"And for why that?"

"He says it was the Jews that had him thrown out of San Francisco."

Rawlings was quiet for a while, turning his head now and then as they grew closer to the dock and he had to con the boat around anchored ships.

Finally he said: "You think that once this is over we'll all be riding in carriages like Warful says?"

"No, I think we'll all be dead," Battles said.

Rawlings again lapsed into a few moments silence, then said: "Thankee for that, Matt. It will help me chart a course a few p'ints off the one I'd intended."

Battles didn't think anything of that remark at the time, but it would have consequences that would imperil them all.

A man with no eyes, no tongue, no nose or ears, trussed up in an iron cage under a blazing sun, covered with flies that feast on his dried blood, welcomes death as a groom welcomes his bride to bed on his wedding night.

And so it was with Luke Anderson.

He had strangled a woman with his bare hands, and justice had been swift, the punishment severe.

Now he groaned in his endless agonies, his entire consciousness turned inward, focused on self . . . wheels within wheels of regret, pain, despair, and the death of hope.

Under the belligerent gaze of the Iron Handmaidens, Battles and Rawlings looked up at the cage, their expressions revealing a mix of horror and pity.

"Jesus, Mary, and Joseph and all the saints in heaven preserve us and save us," the seaman whispered. "They're giving the poor man a terrible death."

Battles nodded. "He wasn't much, but no man deserves to die like that." Then, because he felt that some kind of eulogy was needed, he said: "His name was Luke Anderson and he was good with a gun and he knew the way of cannons." He hesitated, and then added: "May his suffering end soon."

He glanced at the letter in his hand. There was no point in delivering it now.

And that meant . . .

Battles knew what it meant: The deaths of four argumentative old men who had probably not harmed a living soul in their lives.

Chapter 38

A Desperate Plan

"There's nothing more we can do here," Matt Battles said.

He turned and walked back toward the town, away from the palace and the dying thing in the cage.

"Matt, you know what I'm thinking about?" Rawlings said.

"The four old men, at a guess."

"They'll dangle from the yardarm. Warful will see to that."

"Judah, I need a revolver," Battles said, a wild plan forming in his head.

Rawlings said: "Bless your heart, there's plenty of guns for sale in Eugene de Montijo, if you've the money to pay for them."

"American money?"

The seaman smiled. "Any kind of money."

"Then let's find a gun store."

The proprietor of the rod and gun shop was a Levant Arab with predatory eyes who smelled of garlic, gun oil, and treachery.

Battles overpaid for a French service revolver, a double-action, six-shot Chamelot-Delvigne in 11 caliber. He also bought a box of shells, again at an exorbitant price, and Rawlings had to bail him out by throwing five dollars in the pot.

"Damn robber," Battles said when they were out on the street.

Rawlings shook his head. "It's just business as usual in this town. He could tell you needed a gun real bad and he took advantage, lay to that."

Battles smiled and shoved the revolver in his

waistband. "Remind me to come back here and shoot him."

Rawlings's serious expression didn't change. "What are you going to do with that gun?"

"Save the lives of four old men," Battles said. "But I'll need your help, Judah."

"Chart me the course first. If I see no shoals an' I'm still on board with you, I'll let 'er rip."

Battles, using as few words as possible, told him his plan.

And suddenly Rawlings turned white under his tan, like a man with seasickness.

"You're a rough hand, Matt, and no mistake," he said, his voice unsteady. "But it's way too thin."

"Can I depend on you?"

"When you start, there's bound to be a commotion on deck," Rawlings said. "And I'll have two steady lads in the jolly boat, lay to that. But"—he shook his head—"damn me, it's as thin as hen's skin."

"It's all I've got," Battles said.

"Warful's fat lady will never go for it."

"She'll have to," Battles said. "If she doesn't, I'll blow her head off." He smiled. "Lay to that."

The jolly boat was still a distance from the ship when Warful appeared at the rail.

He cupped his hand to his mouth and yelled, "Did you deliver the letter?"

"No," Battles answered. Then, to simplify a shouted exchange: "Luke Anderson is dead."

Warful seemed almost pleased.

"Then, by God, I'll hang the Jews," he yelled.

Battles pulled his shirt over the butt of his revolver, then scrambled up the ship's ladder while Rawlings was still making the boat fast.

He had just set foot on deck when Durango emerged from belowdecks with the four gray-beards, their lips moving in silent prayer.

"An eye for an eye, a tooth for a tooth, is not that the high and dry of it?" Warful said to his assembled gunmen.

There were no murmurs of agreement, and men shuffled their feet or stared down at the deck. The gunmen were outlaws and killers, but each had drawn a line years before over which the tattered remains of his conscience would not allow him to step.

For most, that line was represented by the four harmless old men now silently waiting to be hung from the mizzen yard.

The sailors, though hardened by the rigors of a harsh service, stood back and made no effort to assist Warful. Like the gunmen, they too were drawing a line.

Warful, an unholy joy in his eyes, seemed to dance a little jig as he moved from one man to the next and placed a noose around his neck.

He turned to his men, his mouth wide open in soundless laughter, as though he'd just made a good joke.

"What harm have we ever done to you that you slaughter us like this?" the oldest man said, speaking for the first time since he'd been dragged on deck.

Warful rounded on him, his face savage.

"The fact that your shadow pollutes the earth is harm enough," he said.

The old man said no more. There is no seeking mercy from madmen.

"I'll need help to haul 'em up," Warful said, turning to his men. "But first I must bring my lady wife, who is eager to join in the fun."

Battles jumped at his chance. "I'll get her," he said.

"Thank you, Mr. Battles, most thoughtful," Warful said. "You will haul on a rope as a reward."

The trouble with madmen is that they believe everyone is as crazy as themselves, Battles thought as he headed for the captain's cabin and the eager Mrs. Warful.

The door of the cabin was not locked and Battles barged inside.

An unspeakable stench slammed him and he stopped in his tracks, as though he'd walked into a wall.

At Warful's insistence, the cabin hadn't been

cleaned since the ship had left San Francisco, and the smell of stale vomit and scraps of rotting food added to the woman's vile body odor.

Hattie Warfield enjoyed her dirt, wallowed in filth like a great sow, and her husband either ignored or encouraged her.

She stood at a scrap of mirror in her shift, smearing scarlet rouge on her fat cheeks.

"I'm not ready yet," she said. "Tell Mr. Warful I'll be along directly."

For a moment Battles doubted he could go through with it.

The thought of touching Hattie's gross body revolted him. He felt like running up on deck and gulping clean air into his lungs.

But the lives of four men were at stake and he had to do it.

Hattie was suddenly annoyed. "Do as I told you. Tell Mr. Warful I'll be on deck soon and not to hang the Jews until I get there."

Battles drew the Chamelot-Delvigne, a short-barreled revolver that balanced in the hand as well as a Colt.

He pointed the gun at Hattie. "Outside, now!"

The fat woman was outraged. "What is the meaning of this?"

"Ma'am, the meaning is that if you don't head for the door I'll put a bullet in your hide," Battles said.

"You won't shoot a woman," Hattie said.

"Depends on the woman," Battles said. "Let's go."

194

Chapter 39

A Daring Escape

Matt Battles overcame his revulsion for Hattie Warful and pushed her onto the deck with his arm around her neck, the muzzle of his revolver jammed against her temple.

For the first few moments, everyone stood frozen in place and it seemed to Battles that even the ocean breeze held its breath.

His face registering both shock and horror, Warful was the first to react.

He took a step forward, but again froze when Battles said: "Come any closer, Warful, and I'll scatter her brains."

"He means it, Hatfield," the woman wailed. "He'll kill me. He said he would."

"Beloved!" Warful cried.

He raised a fist at Battles. "Harm a hair of her beautiful head and I'll kill you."

"Take the nooses off those men, Warful," Battles said.

The man hesitated, and Battles said: "Do it now or I'll drop the fat lady dead at your feet."

Battles glanced at the gunmen facing him on the deck. None showed any inclination to intervene, even Durango, who was armed and fast enough to be dangerous.

The marshal wasn't particularly liked by most of the gunmen, but he wasn't particularly disliked either. It seemed to Battles that they were holding pat, as they tried to decide whether or not to make a play.

Hattie's raw stench curling in his nostrils, Battles waited until the four old men were freed from their nooses; then he said: "You, Judah Rawlings," he said, "help these men into the boat."

The seaman played his role to the hilt. "Anything you say, matey," he said, his voice shaking a little. "Just don't shoot."

After the four men were safely in the jolly boat, a pair of burly sailors at the oars Rawlings had promised, Battles backed toward the rail, using Hattie as a shield.

"You'll never reach shore alive, Battles," Warful said. He waved a hand. "All these men are marksmen."

The rail bumped against Battles's waist and, suddenly angry from both fear and stress, he lifted his right leg, put his boot into the fat woman's backside, and pushed hard.

Hattie floundered across the deck, windmilling her fat arms like a cartwheeling she-bear, and then pitched flat onto her face.

Battles scrambled down the ladder and yelled to the seamen at the oars to get the hell away from there.

The sailors must have owed Rawlings a favor or three, because they bent to their task and pulled swiftly away from the *Lila*.

Warful, a gun in his hand, was the first to appear at the rail. He fired, and fired again, but both his shots went wild.

"I fear we have put you in the greatest danger, my friend," Jacob Bensoussan said, his blue eyes concerned.

"Don't worry about me, old-timer," Battles said. "Right now worry about yourself."

The oarsmen were doing their best to put distance between themselves and the *Lila*, but now several gunmen, including Durango, joined Warful at the rail and cut loose.

It was one thing to refuse to participate in the hanging of old men, but taking potshots at a fleeing rowboat was quite another.

Now, that was fun.

But the gunmen were close-range revolver fighters, and to Battles's relief he saw no rifles among them.

A bullet chipped wood near the port oarlock and another kicked up a spurt of water near the bow.

Irritated, Battles double-actioned the French revolver. The trigger was light and smooth, but he was unfamiliar with the weapon and his shots pulled high. But he had the satisfaction of seeing both Warful and Durango duck as his bullets whined over their heads.

The boat was now out of revolver range, but, to Battles's horror, he saw Ben Lane swing the starboard swivel gun in his direction.

The man could fire a cannon, but he wasn't a cannoneer.

If he'd been, he'd have known that the gun hadn't been reloaded since the *Lila* left port and the powder charge was probably damp.

Such was the case. The gun misfired and, robbed of his fun, Lane's curses carried across the water.

Warful danced with rage on the deck, screaming words that sea and distance made impossible to hear.

Matt Battles looked back at the ship, a harsh reality dawning on him. If the *Lila* was his bridge back to the United States, he'd well and truly burned it.

Jacob Bensoussan, looking old and impossibly frail, stood on the dock with Battles, the two seamen lounging nearby.

"You must come home with me," the old man said. "I'm afraid the madman will leave no stone unturned to find you." He smiled. "Over the centuries, Jews have become quite good at hiding themselves and others."

Battles shook his head. "No, I can't do that. I could bring Warful right to your doorstep."

Bensoussan shrugged expressively. "My wife is dead, my children are all gone, I live alone, and I'm ill. What can the madman do to me?"

"Hang you," Battles said. "Or next time use a gun."

"I will take that risk to save your life, as you saved mine."

Battles laid a hand on the old man's skinny shoulder. "Go home. Please. I'll be all right."

Bensoussan realized that further argument was useless.

"Then *zay gezunt*, and may God bless you," he said.

"Thank you," Battles said. "And ride easy, old-timer."

After the old man left, the two sailors stepped to Battles.

The taller one, a good-looking youngster with a topman's muscular shoulders and arms, said, pointing: "Mate, you can find a cozy berth at the Saracens Head Inn, just along the dockside yonder."

"That takes money, and I have none," Battles said.

"My name is Dave Noonan," the sailor said. "Now you go to the inn and find Molly Poteet, then, says you, 'I'm a shipmate o' Dave Noonan's and he said to put my score on the slate.' Then, says you, 'Dave says to never fear, he'll pay the bill later.'"

"Why would you do this?" Battles said, a man recently grown to suspicion.

"For one reason, mate, the way you saved them old galoots from a rope. That was done handsomely, an' no mistake. So says Cap'n Rawlings, and so say I."

"You're gold dust, Mr. Battles," the second man said, smiling.

"I'll take you up on your offer, Noonan," Battles said. "And I'll repay you when I can."

The sailor grinned. "Don't you concern yourself with that, matey. I'll be a rich man soon and there's the cut-an'-dried of it."

"You might be a dead man if Warful thinks we were in cahoots and you helped me escape," Battles said.

"No worry on that score, mate. Take Cap'n Rawlings, now. He has a silver tongue in his head when he wishes, speaks like a chapling, you might say. He'll be telling Warful that we was held at gunpoint an' only rowed the boat to save our lives, lay to that."

Battles held out his hand. "Well, good luck."

"And luck to you too," Noonan said.

But right then, Battles didn't feel lucky.

He didn't feel lucky at all.

Chapter 40

The Saracens Head

"You're telling me that Davy Noonan will pay your score, and I'm a-tellin' you that he's a lying rogue who should've been hung at execution dock years ago or died of the rum or the French pox."

Molly Poteet, plump, pretty, and belligerent, put her fists on her ample hips. "So, what do ye think o' that, Mr. Cowboy, or whatever the hell you be?"

"I'm sorry, ma'am," Battles said, touching his hat. "I meant no harm, and I'll be on my way."

"Wait," Molly said. "You're a man of manners, or at least you've been around them as have them." She scrutinized Battles's face, her eyes lingering on his scars. "Maybe I'll take a chance on you, since you're a fellow American. Are you hungry?"

Battles nodded. "I can't recollect when I last ate a decent meal."

"Well, that's what you'll find here, a decent meal and a clean bed, and a dove to warm it if you so choose."

Battles smiled. "The bed will do just fine." He hesitated, then added: "I'm sure Dave Noonan will pay my score."

"Maybe he will, maybe he won't," Molly said. "We'll see." She beckoned to Battles. "Come with me."

The woman led him into a room at the back of the premises that she kept as her bedroom. There was a pantry against one wall, a bed against the one opposite, and a table and four chairs in the middle of the floor. Two easy chairs by the fireplace and knotted rugs gave the room a cozy feel.

The Saracens Head was a narrow building, a tavern and dining room on the ground floor, bedrooms on the two above. Like all the structures in town, it was a ramshackle, wooden edifice with a sharply steeped gable roof that overhung the street.

Withal, it looked as though a breath of wind could send the whole building crashing down in a pile of shattered timbers and rising dust.

Molly Poteet stepped to the pantry, then turned.

"I can't call you Cowboy," she said. "What do you call yourself?"

Battles gave his name, and the woman said: "How did you end up in this godforsaken place?"

"The ship anchored out there, the *Lila*. I was a . . . passenger."

"Do you have a return passage?"

"I don't really know."

"Is Poke Yates still captain?"

"No. He's dead."

Molly seemed taken aback. "Then I hope he roasts in hell," she said. "I guess Mad Dog Donovan is now master."

"No, he's dead too."

"Mad Dog's been dead before. He keeps coming back."

"Not this time. I shoved a cutlass into his guts, then threw him into the sea."

Molly absorbed that without comment, as though the recounting of violence was an everyday occurrence. She said: "I was Poke Yates's kept woman. He grew tired of me and marooned me here. That was . . . damn, it was ten years ago."

"You've prospered since," Battles said, looking around him.

"I guess so, if being the owner of a cathouse and tavern in a heathen land can be called prospering."

Before Battles could comment, Molly said: "Do you like cheese?"

"Just fine, so long as there's no weevils in it."

"Hardboiled eggs? Do you like those?"

"Sure."

"And how about a dish of cold *samke harra*?"

"You got me there," Battles said, grinning.

Molly smiled. "I thought I would. It's an Arab dish, made with salted, fried fish."

"Begging your pardon, ma'am, but I reckon the cheese and eggs will do just fine," Battles said.

・・・

The woman watched Battles eat for a few minutes, then poured him a glass of wine.

"What are you running from, Matt?" she said.

"Is it that obvious?" Battles said, startled.

"A man with a French pistol in his pants who keeps his eyes on the door is running from something. The law?"

"Here, in this town? What law?"

"You're running nonetheless. Tell me about it. Who knows? I may be able to help you."

"It's long in the telling."

"Fine by me. I've got all day."

Battles sat back in his chair, lit a cigarette, then, being spare with words, told the woman of everything that had happened between his meeting with the president and his rescue of the four old Jewish men.

He was building his fourth cigarette as he finished the story and said: "So, I've failed on all counts. I didn't get in contact with the president to explain the sudden disappearance of the West's most dangerous gunmen, I failed to prevent the theft of the gold, and I couldn't put an end to Hatfield Warful's madness."

"Maybe. But you saved Jacob Bensoussan and his cronies," Molly said. "I set store by those old men. They often come into my tavern to drink a glass of wine and argue about the Torah."

The woman smiled. "Something told me that I should take a chance on you."

She stepped to the door, opened it wide, and yelled: "Hassan!"Almost as though he'd materialized out of thin air, a ragged little Arab urchin appeared at the door.

"Yaz, Miz Molly," he said, grinning from ear to ear.

"Hassan, go down to the dock," the woman said. "If you see a very tall man"—she raised her hand above her head, showing the boy just how tall, Warful was—"you come running back here and tell myself and Mr. Battles."

"Yaz, Miz Molly."

The woman stepped to the pantry, found a red-and-white-striped candy stick, and gave it to the boy.

"Go now," she said.

After the kid left, Battles reloaded the Chamelot-Delvigne, a fairly complicated process that was something of a chore.

But he had no choice.

Something told him he'd need the revolver sooner rather than later.

Chapter 41

Shark Bait

Matt Battles was dozing in one of Molly Poteet's armchairs when the woman burst into the room, Hassan in tow.

"He's on the dock," she said.

Battles woke up fast and jumped to his feet.

"Tell him, Hassan," Molly said.

"Big man," the boy said, and, as the woman had done, he raised his hand, standing on tiptoe. "Like a tree."

"Has he other men with him?" Battles said.

Hassan held up his hands and spread his fingers twice. "That much mens. Look like you," he said. "Big hats."

"There's a vacant room on the top floor, Matt," Molly said. "You can see the dock from there."

Battles followed the woman upstairs and then stepped to the window.

Molly left for a few moments, then returned with a ship's brass telescope. "You'll see better with this," she said.

Battles trained the scope on Warful and even at a distance he saw that the man was still hopping mad. He smiled. That last push he'd given Warful's lady wife had been the final straw.

The gunmen gathered around Warful and he

appeared to be giving them final instructions. A few moments later, they walked away and dispersed into the town.

"They're looking for you all right," Molly said. "I'd better go downstairs and wait for them to show up."

"Molly, I'm beholden to you," Battles said. "I won't forget this."

"Don't fret it, Matt," the woman said. "So far all you owe me is the price of a meal."

After Molly left, Battles again studied Warful.

He sat in a bollard, Durango standing next to him. Warful consulted his watch, said something to the breed, and Durango nodded, his eyes on the teeming main street.

Battles took his gun from his waistband and laid it on the windowsill in front of him.

Then he noticed something . . . strange.

The two big jolly boats that had transferred Warful and his gunmen from the *Lila* had pulled away from the dock and were heading for the ship at a fast clip.

He trained his glass on the *Lila* in time to see the anchor lift from the sea, the flukes and chain dripping water, and sailors were high on the yards, lowering the sails.

The *Lila* was readying for sea.

Acting captain Judah Rawlings was making a run for it.

Battles saw the boats winched on board. Then the bark turned her bow into the northern trade wind, her sails already billowing.

It took a while before Warful noticed what was happening.

But when he did, he acted like a man possessed.

Battles couldn't hear from that distance, but Warful sprinted up and down the dock, waving his arms, his head back, mouth open in what had to be a string of curses.

Durango pulled his gun, but the *Lila* was out of range and he didn't make any attempt to fire.

Warful ran to the gunman, grabbed him by the front of his shirt, and shook him, ordering him to do something, anything.

There were many tall ships and oceangoing dhows tied up at the dock, but none small enough or nimble enough to catch the *Lila*.

The bark was tacking into the wind, now a rifle shot from shore.

Then the unthinkable happened.

It was an act of violence that left Battles shaken to the core so badly that the telescope shook in his suddenly unsteady hands.

The *Lila*'s crew was about to toss shark bait over the side.

Chapter 42

Betrayed!

Matt Battles trained his glass on the *Lila*'s deck and watched in horror as Hattie Warful was dragged to the rail.

The woman was wearing only a shift and her great, sagging body bulged and moved like pigs fighting in a sack.

Grinning sailors ripped away the shift, then manhandled the now-naked woman over the rail and let her go.

Men pumped the air with their fists, jeering, as the gross white body hit the sea with a mighty splash.

For a few moments Hattie floundered in the water like a stranded whale, but then, to Battles's surprise, she recovered and struck out for shore, swimming strongly.

Sailors are a fickle bunch, and soon their jeers turned to cheers, as they encouraged the fat woman to go for it.

She'd stroked maybe twenty-five yards when the first shark struck.

Appalled, yet fascinated, Battles kept the glass glued to his eye.

The shark had bumped Hattie, and she stopped, treading water, looking around her.

A few moments later, the second attack was much more ferocious.

The shark attack drove upward, from under the woman, hitting with such speed and impact that she was hurled high out of the water. Hattie hung motionless in the air for a split second, then cartwheeled back into the sea.

Another hit, and the woman's upper body, her great breasts swinging, surged upward. This time blood fountained around her and arced in a scarlet fan above her head.

Hattie disappeared under the water. After what seemed to Battles an eternity, she broke the surface again. But this time her left breast and arm were missing, leaving only raw meat and shards of white bone.

She sank once more, and this time she didn't reappear.

The *Lila* was now far out to sea, and Battles shifted his attention to Warful.

The man had witnessed the slaughter of his lady wife, and he stood on the dock, staring out at the water, unmoving.

Durango stepped close and said something, but Warful did not react.

He kept his gaze turned to the sea, like a man staring down an empty, leaf-tossed road, waiting in vain for his lover to appear.

Battles lowered the telescope and rubbed

feeling back to his eye socket. It was only then he became aware that Molly Poteet stood behind him.

"I'm sorry I saw it," she said. "Nobody deserves to die that way."

Battles nodded. "She surely died hard."

The woman stood closer to the window and looked at the dock.

"What will he do now?" she said.

"I don't know." Battles shook his head. "He's crazy, so I really don't know what he'll do."

"The ship is gone and with it the gold," Molly said.

"Seems like."

The woman turned and looked at Battles. "What will you do?"

"I don't know that either."

"Maybe you'll stay on at Eugene de Montijo."

"And do what? I'm a lawman. It's all I know. I'd be no good at anything else." He smiled. "Besides, I'm also an American and when my time comes I want to be planted in my own soil."

Battles looked down at the dock. Warful still hadn't moved, standing still, like a stone statue.

After thinking for a while, he said: "I reckon Warful will do one of two things: The death of his wife could drive him so insane, he'll be incapable of doing anything at all."

"And the other?" Molly asked, after a silence.

"He'll go through with his plan to become king of this . . . whatever it is."

Battles smiled. "Of course his hired guns and King Brukwe will have something to say about that."

"Men will fight for treasure," Molly said.

"That's the carrot Warful is dangling in front of them," Battles said.

The woman smiled. "Except there is no treasure and never was."

Molly Poteet read the puzzled expression on Battles's face and said: "Matt, there is no King Brukwe. He died years ago and the French put their own man in his place, a small-time, crooked bureaucrat by the name of Marcel Toucey."

The woman waved Battles into a chair at a table close to the window, and sat on the one opposite.

"All those tales you've heard about Brukwe being winched onto his women, or the Iron Handmaidens committing suicide to show their loyalty, is just that—sailors' tales."

"You mean, Toucey rules the whole shebang?"

"Yes, but under French supervision and they make him account for every cent. Eugene de Montijo is a gold mine, and Paris wants to make sure its entire cut keeps coming. The soldiers and the Iron Handmaidens are paid with French francs to keep the peace and make sure everybody pays their taxes."

Molly pushed a stray curl of brunette hair from her forehead.

"When someone refuses to pay the French their dues, he's put in the cage as an example to others," she said. "But King Brukwe is a convenient scapegoat for French ruthlessness, so they're happy to keep alive the myth that he exists."

"Damn, that's why there were no Afrikaners," Battles said. "Toucey never tried to hire them. He wanted a share of the gold all right and pretended to go along with Warful's crazy scheme, but at little risk to himself. And the reason Durango failed to find him was that he couldn't search the palace."

"Toucey lives in the palace all right, but not like a king. He has an office and from there he runs the port to the advantage of French West Africa."

"The profit from slavery is dirty money," Battles said. "I'm surprised the French accept it."

"Officially they don't," Molly said, "at least as far as Europe is concerned. What happens in Africa is a whole different story. The lives of black natives don't count for much, and slavery has always helped finance empire building."

Battles rose, stepped to the window, and trained the glass on Warful.

The man still stood, staring out to sea. But now he'd been joined by half a dozen gunmen who were talking with Durango.

They looked like a crestfallen bunch.

"Nothing happening down there," Battles said. "It seems like—"

The words died in his throat as feet pounded on the stairs and the door to the room burst open.

"There he is!" Hassan yelled, pointing to Battles.

Chapter 43

A Sea Chase

Matt Battles went for the gun on the windowsill, but Marcel Toucey's voice stopped him.

"I wouldn't, Mr. Battles," he said. "My men can cut you down right where you stand."

Battles's hand froze and he turned slowly.

Marcel Toucey, flanked by two of his soldiers with bayonets fixed, stood in the middle of the floor.

"You will come with me, Mr. Battles," the Frenchman said. "Now."

"And if I don't?"

"I'll kill you."

Molly Poteet glared at Hassan. "You little weasel."

"Don't blame the boy," Toucey said. "He is one of my spies and was only doing his duty."

"Damn it, Toucey, the man you want is down there at the dock," Battles said. "He plans to be king here, not me."

"Yes, yes, I know, become king and kill all the Jews. He told me. But at the moment I need you, not Monsieur Warful."

"Need me for what?"

"Later." Toucey waved a hand toward the door. "Please, come with me. And you may bring your revolver, if it pleases you."

It pleased Battles. He stuck the gun in his waistband and followed Toucey downstairs. Behind him he was aware of Molly wringing her hands and looking distraught.

For some reason Battles was happy that it wasn't the woman who'd betrayed him.

Toucey led the way to a section of the dock that was cordoned off by at least fifty soldiers. Warful and his gunmen stood only yards away, but the Frenchman ignored them, though Battles was aware of hard stares from Durango, Lon Stuart, and others.

As for Warful, he looked neither to his left nor right, gazing out at the turquoise sea where the quick, gleaming sharks glided.

Prodded by bayonets, Battles boarded a flatiron gunboat with a massive, twelve-inch cannon mounted in the bow. There was no rigging, but twin screws could drive the boat at a steady nine knots and it carried a crew of thirty, all of them bare-chested natives with a single white officer in command.

Toucey barked a command and the gunboat cast off, her screws churning as she reversed from the dock and then pointed her bow seaward. The Frenchman beckoned Battles to join him near the cannon's armored shield forward where the racket of the steam engines was less.

"Captain Rawlings thinks very highly of you," Toucey said. "Or so I'm reliably informed. Is this the case?"

"We weren't exactly huggin' kin," Battles said. "But we got along."

"Good, because you will help me talk Rawlings out of this present madness and return to port." He turned and looked at Battles. "That's one reason I didn't shoot you out of hand."

"Shoot me, but let Warful go?"

"No, I'll deal with the madman on our return."

The Frenchman was silent for a while, studying the choppy sea ahead of him. As yet, there was no sign of the *Lila*.

Finally Toucey said: "There's another reason I didn't want to kill you, Mr. Battles, though I believe you are as big a rogue as Warful and the rest."

"My good looks and sparkling personality?" Battles said, not liking this man.

"You saved the life of Rabbi Jacob Bensoussan," Toucey said. "The old man is very dear to me and I appreciate his wisdom. He says

216

you saved him from the madman's rope, he and three others."

Battles nodded. "Warful planned to hang them because they were Jews. I couldn't stand by and let that happen."

Toucey shook his head. "Where does it spring from, this hatred of Jews?"

"I can't answer that, but in Warful's case he says they were jealous of his business success and had him thrown out of San Francisco."

"So he made Jews a scapegoat for his own failures?"

"Seems like."

"Then thank God that kind of mad thinking is confined to America and will never take hold in Europe," Toucey said.

The gunboat made fast progress, and Toucey ordered the big gun at the bow loaded, expecting he'd overhaul the *Lila* soon.

Despite the lowering sun, the day was hot and the sea breeze that streamed the tricolor at the stern did little to cool the deck.

An hour after the boat left port, the forward lookout took a telescope from his eye and yelled something in French and Toucey said to the officer: *"Le Lieutenant Laurent, tenez-vous prêt votre fusil."*

Toucey turned to Battles. "The *Lila* is in sight and I ordered Laurent to stand by his gun. She's under full sail and she's got half a league in hand, but we'll catch her, never fear."

The Frenchman looked through his glass and after a moment said: "There, she's flung aloft her royals and she's flying fair to the wind."

Battles scanned the horizon, but because of the haze, he saw nothing but a pale blue expanse of sea and sky.

Toucey called for more speed, but the engineer shrugged and spread his hands. The gunboat's boiler seams were already strained, and the possibility of an explosion was an ever-present danger.

The sun hung like a copper coin in the sky and was setting fast, and Toucey kept casting worried glances at the western horizon.

The gunboat was not equipped for a night action, and if he didn't overtake the bark soon he'd lose her in the dark.

The *Lila* was visible now. There was only a mile of sea between her and the gunboat, and the Frenchman did a little jig of anxiety on the deck.

"Lieutenant Laurent, can you do anything with the gun?" he said finally.

The young officer stared at the *Lila*, as the roughening sea threw spray over the gunboat's bow.

"The range is extreme, sir," Laurent said, his face streaming water. "But I'm willing to give it a try."

"Then do it," Toucey said.

This exchange was in French, a language Battles did not understand, but he caught the gist when Laurent barked orders and the gun crew scrambled to the cannon.

The big gun was fixed to the boat's deck and could not be moved latterly, but it was capable of being elevated.

"Across her bow, Lieutenant, if you please," Toucey said.

The big gun roared and the recoil almost brought the tiny gunboat to a shuddering halt.

Battles watched for the fall of shot, and a moment later saw an exclamation point of white water erupt about fifty yards abaft the *Lila*'s stern.

"Once again, if you please," Toucey said. "Across her bow."

The day shaded to lilac as the sun lowered and to the north a single star heralded the coming of night.

"You're running out of daylight, Toucey," Battles said.

"Never fear," the Frenchman said. "We'll find the range soon."

Chapter 44

Slaughter on the Deck

The gunboat's cannon fired again, spiking flame and sparks. The sixteen-inch ball splashed into the sea about twenty yards off the *Lila*'s starboard beam.

"Once again, if you please," Toucey said.

The gun crew, soaked by flaying spray, reloaded quickly. The helmsman pointed the gunboat's bow forward of the *Lila* and the cannon boomed.

This time the ball threw up a tower of water as high as the bark's mizzen, just a few yards ahead of her bow.

It was enough.

The *Lila*'s royals came down as crewmen swarmed the yards. A short while later, the bark struck her colors. As the Stars and Stripes lowered, the men on the gunboat cheered.

The bark lost speed, but drifted slowly to the north, driven by the hard-blowing trade wind.

"Bring her in close," Toucey said. "Handsomely, now."

The gunboat approached the *Lila*'s starboard side, most of her native crew now carrying rifles.

When she was within hailing distance, Toucey

yelled in English: "A word with Captain Rawlings, if you please."

Men milled about on the *Lila*'s deck, but Rawlings didn't show at the rail. Throttled back to a crawl, the gunboat rocked in the rising sea and Battles spread his legs wide as he fought to keep his balance on the heaving deck.

The light was almost gone, the sun now a fast-fading memory.

Toucey stood at the gunboat's bow, cupped his hands to his mouth, his head thrown back. "Prepare to be boarded," he yelled.

Battles saw it coming.

But he was stunned by its audacity. Or lunacy.

The starboard swivel gun on the quarterdeck was manned by Judah Rawlings and a seaman. And it was trained on the gunboat.

"Down!" Battles yelled.

He dived for the deck just as the gun fired.

A round of canister swept the boat deck. Iron balls the size of walnuts ricocheted off steel and embedded in flesh.

Battles saw Toucey and the lieutenant go down, as well as half a dozen crewmen. Blood, brain, and bone splattered around him and men screamed.

A cheer went up from the *Lila* as the grinning Rawlings reloaded his gun.

Horribly wounded, his face a grotesque scarlet

mask, Lieutenant Laurent struggled to his knees.

As Battles watched, amazed that there was still life in the officer's shattered body, Laurent reached up and yanked the bow cannon's lanyard.

The effect was devastating.

The huge ball smashed into the *Lila*'s side and shattered its way clean through her timbers. Flying splinters of pine and oak killed and maimed men on her deck, and Battles was sure he saw Dave Noonan go down.

Driven back by the recoil of her cannon, the gunboat was separated from the *Lila* by ten yards of sea. The bark suddenly took a forty-five-degree list to her starboard as she took in tons of water.

Like a nervous belle at her first ball, the *Lila* swooned, and her foremast crashed onto the gunboat's deck in a tangle of rigging and canvas, injuring more of Toucey's crewmen.

Battles extricated himself from under a sail and then stood—in time to see the bark start to go under by the bow. For a moment her dripping stern hung above the waves, and then it too slid into the sea.

The *Lila* was gone . . . taking with her many a lively sailor lad and a fortune in stolen gold.

Ten or twelve of the bark's crewmen splashed around in the water, crying out for help. But the gunboat's native seamen, enraged at the bloody deaths of so many of their shipmates and what they saw as Rawlings's treachery, were in no mood to take prisoners.

They raised their rifles and shot the floundering seamen like ducks in a pond.

Battles saw Rawlings take a bullet in the head. Then the man threw up his arms and went under.

Soon there was no one alive in the sea, and the water was stained with heaving clouds of crimson.

Within moments the black-eyed sharks came.

Chapter 45

Battles Struggles with His Conscience

The steel deck was slippery with blood as Matt Battles made his way forward. The canister shot, fired at point-blank range into the boat's crowded deck, had done great execution, and at least five men were dead and that many injured.

When he reached the gun, Battles saw at a glance that the lieutenant was dead, his entire lower jaw shot away. The young naval officer's bravery would go unnoticed and only his family in far-off France would grieve for him.

A ball, probably the same one that had killed Laurent, had grazed Marcel Toucey's forehead. The man was groggy, streaming blood, but he was alive, looking around him with unfocused eyes.

Battles kneeled next to him, and the Frenchman stared at him for a long time before his vision cleared and recognition dawned in his face.

"The *Lila*?" he said.

"She's gone. Sunk." Then, lest any blame fall on the native crew, he added: "With all hands. Drownin' is a sure cure for sailor rannies with bad habits."

Toucey blinked and said: "The gold?"

"At the bottom of the sea."

The Frenchman was dazed and Battles helped him to his feet.

He stood swaying for a moment, looking around in horror at the slaughter on the deck.

"This wasn't my fault," he said. "All I wanted was my fair share, nothing more." He sounded like a repentant sinner in a confessional.

"Man has to get used to disappointments, I guess," the marshal said.

"It's dark," Toucey said. "All of a sudden it's dark."

"Seems like," Battles said. "I guess we should turn this tub around and get back to the dock."

The engineer was still alive and Toucey gave him the order.

As the gunboat turned her bow toward the land, the Frenchman rubbed his aching head and said: "I wanted to wear a top hat and ride along the Champs-Élysées in a carriage."

Matt Battles looked out at the ink-dark sea and said nothing.

A man has to repair his own broken dreams.

When the gunboat docked, Toucey was surrounded by soldiers and hustled away. The dead and wounded were carried off the blood-slick boat and they too were taken into the town.

Battles walked the dock, but saw no sign of Hatfield Warful or his gunmen.

He stopped and took time to build and light a cigarette before trying to figure Warful's next move.

Now that he and his men were stranded far from home, all that was left to them was the lure of King Brukwe's treasure, a mythical fortune that had never existed.

Would Warful try to take the palace and put himself on the throne with just sixteen or seventeen men, skilled and ruthless gunfighters though they were?

Would the French merely shrug and let it happen?

And what of himself? Somehow he had to get back home and make his report to President Arthur—for what it was worth.

Would the president be delighted that twenty of the West's most dangerous outlaws and gunmen now lay dead and buried in African soil?

Would he even remember or still care?

Battles had plenty of questions and no answers. He took a final drag of his cigarette and ground out the butt under his heel.

Right now he needed a drink.

"You need a drink, Matt," Molly Poteet said.

The woman poured bourbon into a glass. "You've got blood on your face."

"It's not mine," Battles said.

Molly stepped to the dresser and poured water from a pitcher into the bowl. She wet a washcloth and wiped the blood from Battles's face.

"I wasn't real sure I'd see you alive again," she said, looking at the cloth that was now stained pink.

Battles drained his glass and the woman refilled it.

"If it wasn't for the contrariness of cannonballs, I would be," Battles said. "Dead, I mean."

"What happened out there?" Molly said.

"Madness," Battles said.

And he told Molly Poteet the story.

When he was finished, she said: "What happens now?"

"I wish I knew. I reckon—"

Someone knocked at the parlor door, and it swung open, letting in a clamor of talk, laughter, and piano music from the tavern. A black man wearing a bartender's apron stepped inside and said: "Begging your pardon, Miz Molly, but four French army officers want credit until payday. What do I say?"

"You say yes," Molly said. "They're good for it."

After the man left, Battles said: "French army officers?"

"Yes, from the regiment stationed just across the border. They come in quite often, including their colonel, for a drink and sometimes a woman."

"How about the enlisted men, are they native levies?"

Molly shook her head. "No, they're white soldiers." The woman thought for a moment and added: "I remember Colonel Blanchard, a proud-talking man, telling someone that he commands the best regiment of line infantry in the world."

She looked at Battles, puzzled. "Why are you so interested in French soldiers?"

"Because if Warful tries to take the palace and the French intervene, a regular infantry regiment will cut him and his men to pieces."

The puzzled expression didn't leave Molly's face. "Matt, why do you care?"

Battles hesitated and then said: "I don't know. I don't give a damn if Warful dies, but the rest . . . well, they're my fellow Americans and when you come right down to it, we're in the same business, only on opposite sides. Maybe in the end it boils down to professional courtesy . . . or that I can't idly stand by and see men slaughtered because of a madman's fantasy."

"You owe those gunmen nothing, Matt, nothing at all. Let them get killed."

Battles shook his head. "I can't let them die needlessly. Don't ask me why, but I . . . just . . . can't . . . do . . . it."

"Then you're a fool."

"I know that," Battles said. "Nobody knows that better than me."

Battles lay in bed in the room overlooking the dock. The moon bladed through the window and cast a cross-shaped shadow on the opposite wall.

He heard the bedroom door creak and reached for the revolver on the table beside him.

"Don't shoot, Matt," Molly Poteet said.

She stood by the bed and dropped her shift, leaving her naked body bathed in moonlight.

"Will you send me away?" she said.

"No," Battles said, the word husking in his throat. "I reckon not."

The woman slipped into bed beside him.

"It's been a while," Battles said. "Maybe I've forgotten how it's done."

"I'll remind you," Molly said before her mouth met his.

Chapter 46

Durango's Warning

Next morning Matt Battles sat in the dining room eating breakfast when he was joined by the two men he least expected to see.

Durango and Lon Stuart pulled up chairs and sat opposite him, neither with a gun showing.

"How's it going, Matt?" Durango said. The breed was smiling, always a warning sign with gunmen of his kind.

"I'm doing just fine," Battles said. "You?"

"Fine, Matt. Just fine."

Battles laid his fork on the plate, his appetite fled.

"You know the *Lila* is gone?" he said. "The gold's at the bottom of the Atlantic."

"Heard that," Lon Stuart said. "And I heard tell you saw the whole thing."

"Uh-huh. I was on the gunboat that sank her."

"Matt, we need to talk," Durango said.

"That's what we're doing, ain't it?"

"Not chatter. War talk. Deep talk. About the king's treasure."

"Did Warful send you here?"

Durango hesitated, blinking, then said: "Hat wants to bury the hatchet, let bygones be bygones." He picked up Battles's fork, speared a piece of pork, and put it in his mouth. Chewing, he said: "You seen what happened to his lady wife?"

"I saw it."

"He's all cut up about that. He's hardly the same man anymore."

"He still want to be king?"

"Yeah, he does."

"Then he's the same man."

Stuart turned as a waiter stepped past. "Hey, boy," he said. "Bring us more coffee here, chop-chop, huh?"

The man flashed Stuart a white grin. "Right away, sah."

Stuart directed his attention back to Battles.

"We got it all figured," he said. "Last night we talked with the captain of a Dutch trading sloop. He says he's willing to take us on board and drop us off farther down the coast, maybe the German colony. We'll be so rich by then, we can pay a boat captain to take all of us back to the good ol' U.S. of A."

Durango said: "The way I see us playing it, we gun our way into the palace, leave Warful a-settin' on the throne, and then head for the dock with the treasure. It's an in-and-out job, Matt. Fast, real fast. In, grab the treasure. Out, skedaddle to the dock and the waiting boat."

Stuart said: "Can't be more simple than that. Sure, we'll lose a few men, but it means a bigger share for them of us that are still alive."

● ● ●

The waiter laid cups and a china coffeepot on the table.

When the man moved away again, Durango leaned forward so his face was closer to Battles.

"We need your gun, Matt," he said. "Say it plain now: Will you join us?"

Battles watched Stuart pour himself coffee, then took the pot and filled his own cup. Finally he said: "There is no treasure and there is no King Brukwe. The only person living in the palace is Marcel Toucey, and he's a clerk for the French government."

Battles's statement was greeted by a prolonged silence.

"Then you're agin us," Durango finally said, slamming back in his chair. "Lying to us to protect your French friends."

Battles shook his head. "Durango, I'm not for you or agin you, and the only people I'm trying to protect are you and the others. I don't want to see all of you killed for a treasure that doesn't exist except in Hatfield Warful's mind."

"Who's paying you?" Durango said, pushing it. "Is it Toucey?"

"Nobody's paying me. Hell, I can't even ante up for this breakfast. The man who said he'd stake me went down with the *Lila*."

"You're lying to protect somebody, maybe even the damned king," Durango said. "There's

231

treasure in the palace, enough to make us all rich. You know it, and I know it."

Battles kept his mouth shut. Durango's mind was made up and nothing he could say would change it.

Stuart took time to drain his cup. Then he stood.

"Battles," he said, "I told you once before, I was born and raised in hell and I make a real bad enemy."

"I'm not your enemy, Lon," the marshal said. "Warful is."

"Then join us, damn you."

Battles shook his head. "You're chasing shadows, but you'll do it without me."

Durango jumped to his feet.

"Matt, then stay in this hellhole and rot," he said. "A man doesn't get second chances with me."

He and Stuart stepped to the door, but Durango turned and said: "Take a word of advice. From now on don't let our paths cross in the street unless you're heeled."

Chapter 47

A Pact with the Devil

"When do you think they'll attack the palace?" Molly Poteet said.

"I don't know," Battles said. "Soon, I guess."

"There's no stopping them?"

"No. They're convinced there's treasure. Maybe if the *Lila* hadn't sunk and was still in port, Durango would've listened to reason and settled for the gold on board. But now the treasure is all he's got and he's grabbing at it like a drowning man clutching at a feather."

"You tried, Matt," Molly said. "You've done all you can."

"Seems like," Battles said.

It was an unsatisfactory answer and the woman pushed it.

"Since when does a lawman care so much about outlaws and killers?"

"Because if there were no outlaws and killers, there would be no lawmen." Battles grinned. "And star-strutters like me would be plumb out of business."

Someone knocked lightly on the parlor door and then it creaked open.

Hassan stepped inside, his face split in a huge grin.

"What do you want, you little sneak?" Molly said.

The boy's grin widened. He ran to Molly and grabbed her hand.

"Come see," he said. He made the tall gesture. "Big man outside with coffin, peoples crying. You'll see."

Battles got to his feet, his hand dropping to the butt of his gun.

"How many men with him, Hassan?" he said.

"No men. Just womens." Now he ran and grabbed Battles's hand. "Come see."

Molly got to her feet. "I suppose I should go see what he's talking about."

"I'll come with you," Battles said.

Warful and his coffin had already passed the Saracens Head, and Battles and Molly followed Hassan farther along the street.

They passed a bunch of woman, a few black but mostly Arab, who wailed, lamented, and tore at their clothes as they sang the praises of the deceased.

"Hired mourners," Molly said. "A sight we see often in this town."

Six native men carried an ornate coffin on their shoulders, draped with black crepe. Warful walked in front, wailing louder than anyone else, tears running down his skull face. He'd acquired a broadcloth suit, several sizes too small for him, and a new tile hat.

In his hands, held high in front of him, he bore a placard that read:

MURDERED
BY
JEWS

Warful raised a hand and stopped the procession; then he yelled to the gawking crowd: "My lady wife is gone! The most beautiful, most wonderful woman in the world, thrown to sharks by the Jewish enemy!"

Most of the grinning onlookers couldn't understand the sign or Warful's English, but they cheered or jeered, depending on their inclination.

A knot of drunken English sailors shouted: "Up with the workers, mate!" and "Down with the aristocracy!" But their comments were so off target that Warful chose to ignore them.

He waved the procession forward and led the pallbearers and shrieking, mourning women with a stately step, holding his vile banner high.

"Where the hell is he headed?" Battles asked Molly.

"The old graveyard on the edge of town," she said.

"He's going to bury an empty coffin?"

"Well, he can hardly bury her in the shark that swallowed her, can he?" Molly said.

Out of what they willingly recognized as morbid curiosity, Battles and Molly followed the funeral procession to the cemetery. An overgrown, treeless tract of ground, its tumbled headstones lay like dead soldiers on an ancient battlefield.

A hole had already been dug, and one of the gravediggers picked yellow bones out of the dirt pile and tossed them away.

The pallbearers none too gently dropped the coffin beside the grave, and the hired mourners increased the volume of their lamentations.

Not to be outdone, Warful vented his grief in a series of wails and heartrending cries and threw himself, sobbing, on top of the coffin, hugging the polished timber with his arms spread wide as though embracing his wife.

Then he lay still in that posture, a man paralyzed with grief.

The mourners, figuring they'd now earned their wages, began to drift away and Battles and Molly joined them.

Warful's fragile sanity was now shattered and the man would be capable of any lunacy, any violence.

Battles made up his mind.

When it came right down to it, he was still a man sworn to uphold the laws of civilization, even in darkest Africa.

It was time to make a pact with the devil.

Chapter 48

Toucey Turns a Deaf Ear

"Matt, Marcel Toucey is a shifty little rodent," Molly said. "You can't trust the man."

"I know that, but I don't have any choice," Battles said. "The only way to prevent needless bloodshed is to get the French involved."

He read the doubt in Molly's face and said: "Warful is completely insane. If he attacks the palace a lot of people will die. I've decided it's my duty as a man and a peace officer to stop him."

"It's Toucey's duty to stop him, not yours."

"He'll stop Warful with guns. If I stand back, do nothing, and watch Americans massacred, I could never again hold up my head in the company of men."

"I said it before, Matt, and I say it again," Molly said. "You're a fool. You're risking your life for a bunch of outlaw riffraff."

"And, as I said before, I agree with you."

The woman stepped to her cupboard and came back to the table with a bottle and a couple of glasses.

"I'm coming with you," she said. "Toucey owes me favors from way back."

"It's too dangerous, Molly," Battles said. "This is not your fight."

The woman poured bourbon for them both.

"Cheers," she said, holding up her glass. "Some liquid courage will do us good."

Battles drank, but he said: "I mean it, Molly. I'm going this alone."

"Just try and stop me," the woman said.

Battles and Molly Poteet jostled their way through the teeming main boulevard, fighting off street urchins who offered to sell them anything from carved wooden elephants to their sister.

The main palace entrance was guarded by Iron Handmaidens as before, and what was left of Luke Anderson still hung in the cage.

"Stay right here and let me do the talking," Molly said. "They know me."

Arguing with Molly was a waste of breath, and Battles did as he was told.

He watched from a distance as the women spoke with the guards, tall, aggressive Amazons who crowded around her and bared their teeth in what Battles hoped were smiles.

After a few minutes and much coming and going by the Handmaidens, Molly waved Battles to her side.

"They say Monsieur Toucey is recuperating from his wounds, but he's agreed to see us," Molly said.

"Nice of him," Battles said.

• • •

A guard waved them toward the door, and once inside, Battles found himself in a huge marble hallway, an elegant grand staircase directly in front of him. Among a forest of potted plants, statues and busts of great Frenchmen stared at Battles with stone eyes, and Napoleon scowled at him.

The Handmaiden led the way to a door at the left of the stair. She knocked, opened the door, and motioned them inside.

Toucey sat behind a small desk in a small room with a small window, indicating that the French colonial powers held him in small esteem.

The man had a fat bandage on his head and a frown on his face.

"I'd rather hoped, Mr. Battles, that I wouldn't see you again until the day I hung you," he said. He looked at Molly. "Good morning, Mademoiselle Potcct. You keep rough company."

Battles felt his spirits sink. Now that the *Lila* was gone, it seemed that Toucey had no further use for him except as gallows bait.

The Frenchman regarded Battles with scant enthusiasm.

"What can I do for you?" he said, his voice flat.

"How's your head?" Battles said, in a desperate and pathetic attempt to be ingratiating.

"It hurts. What can I do for you?"

Battles gathered his thoughts, then said: "I

believe this palace will soon come under attack by Hatfield Warful and his hired gunmen."

"Then he's a fool," Toucey said. "This palace is French soil, and I only have to call out my soldiers to end his adventurism."

"I know, but a lot of men will die, Warful's and yours."

Toucey shrugged. "That is war, monsieur. Men die."

"Call in the French army regiment and we can end this thing before it even gets started. Warful is your enemy, not the men with him."

"They are hired mercenaries, are they not? You will find we French have a short way with mercenaries—the rope or the firing squad."

"Damn it, Toucey, have your men surround the palace now," Battles said. "A show of force could convince Warful, insane though he is, that he doesn't stand a chance of taking the palace."

Toucey took his time, even stopping to light a cigar.

"If and when I am attacked, I'll call out my troops, never fear," he said. He bent his head to a paper on his desk. "Thank you for the warning. Now, if you'll excuse me, I have work to do."

Battles felt like a drover attempting to turn a stampeding herd before it reaches the cliff.

Then he recalled hearing some pompous windbag of a politician declare that, "Desperate times require desperate measures."

Well, the times were desperate, no question about that.

He pulled his French revolver from his waistband and pointed it at the Frenchman's bandaged head.

"On your feet, Toucey," he said. "Or I'll scatter your brains all over the desk."

Chapter 49

Butcher Blanchard

Marcel Toucey sprang to his feet, his eyes red with anger.

"This is an outrage you'll regret," he said. "I'll have you caged for this."

"Toucey," Battles said, "I'm not a regretting man. Now get over here. Me and you are gonna get real close, like kissin' cousins, you might say."

Molly Poteet was horrified. "Matt, what are you doing?"

"Nothing much," Battles said. "I'm just about to start a war with the French empire is all."

"You're insane," Toucey said, spluttering his words.

"I told you before to get over here, Toucey," Battles said. "I'm not a man who likes repeating himself."

The Frenchman saw something cold in Battles's

241

eyes he didn't like. He walked around the desk, and then winced as the marshal shoved the muzzle of his revolver into his belly.

"You're going to shoot a cannon for me," Battles said.

Toucey's face registered puzzlement, then shock.

"I don't know how to shoot a cannon," he said.

"Then find me somebody who does," Battles said.

"Never!" Toucey said. "I will die before I'll betray my country."

"Fine," Battles said. He shoved the muzzle of the revolver against the Frenchman's temple and thumbed back the hammer. "Say good night, Marcel," he said.

"Wait!" Toucey wailed. "Perhaps I can live with a small act of betrayal."

"I knew you would see it my way in the end," Battles said.

He motioned with the revolver. "Go to the door and call for your cannoneer." Battles turned to Molly. "Do you speak French?"

"A little."

"Then make sure Toucey calls for a man to shoot a cannon, and not for a man to shoot us."

"I will do exactly as you told me to do, monsieur," the Frenchman said. "Your little moment of triumph will not last very long. Soon it will be my turn to deal the cards."

Toucey stepped to the door, Battles right behind him, his revolver jammed into the small of the Frenchman's back.

Toucey opened the door and called out something in French. A few moments later, a Handmaiden appeared, a bayoneted rifle in her hands.

Battles felt a surge of panic, but Toucey quickly said something else and the woman left, flouncing a little, her generous hips swaying under her leather skirt.

"I ordered her to bring my *capitaine d'artillerie*," Toucey said. "His name is Viktor Mabuza, and he's a first-rate cannon shot."

Battles looked at Molly and she nodded. "That's what he said."

"Does this man speak English?" Battles asked.

"No," Toucey said. "He speaks French and a little German."

"All right, here's what I want you to tell him," Battles said. "I want him to load a cannon with a ball and train it on the biggest tent in the French army camp, the one with the flag flying over it."

Toucey was appalled. "But that is the tent of Colonel Blanchard, a brave French officer," he said. "He will be eating lunch at this time."

"Good," Battles said. "I plan to feed him a nice hot cannonball."

"You're mad," the Frenchman said. "And your madness will be the death of us all."

Toucey, an emotional man, began to wail that he'd be hung for treason, and Molly, as shocked as the little Frenchman, said: "Matt, do you know what the hell you're doing?"

"You bet." Battles grinned. "I've declared war on the French empire."

Captain Viktor Mabuza was a tall, handsome mulatto, his blue and red uniform impeccable. Unlike the enlisted men he wore knee boots in the French style and his kepi boasted an ostrich feather plume.

"Tell him," Battles told Toucey.

The soldier looked totally baffled, his eyes shifting back and forth between Toucey, Battles, and Molly.

"I can't do this, monsieur," Toucey said. "Colonel Blanchard will hang me for sure."

"And if you don't I'll shoot you," Battles said shoving the gun harder into the man's back. "Only my way will be quicker."

Toucey's jowly face sagged, like a man already walking up the steps to the gallows. He began to speak rapidly in French to the captain, and Molly moved closer, listening intently.

When Toucey stopped speaking, Battles said: "Tell the captain to just aim the cannon. I don't want him to shoot the damned thing until I get there."

The Frenchman spoke again and again Molly listened.

"Sound all right to you?" Battles asked the woman.

"I caught the gist of it," Molly said. "I'm sure he leveled with you."

Captain Mabuza saluted and left and Toucey wheeled on Battles.

"If you fire the cannon, the colonel will hang everyone," he said. "His officers call him Butcher Blanchard because he rejoices in killing prisoners."

Battles ignored the man, but realized all too well that he was rolling the dice.

If his war with France didn't go as planned, Blanchard might indeed hang him, and probably Molly with him.

Then the outburst of shooting he heard from outside told him it was too late anyway.

He'd thrown snake eyes.

Chapter 50

A Thunder of Gunfire

"What is happening?" Marcel Toucey demanded, his eyes wild.

"It's Warful," Battles said. "The fools finally joined him in his madness."

The marshal ran to the door and threw it open.

He saw a Handmaiden go down, blood splashing over her breasts. Screaming her rage, she joined the lanky bodies of two other women on the marble floor.

Several Handmaidens, rifles at a high port, rushed the palace doorway, only to immediately fall to a rolling thunder of gunfire. The expert Colt-handling of Warful's men was taking its toll.

From outside, a Gatling gun, sounding like an iron bedstead dragged across a rough pine floor, chattered briefly, then fell silent.

Battles slammed the door shut.

"Is there another way out of this room?" he said.

"This way," Toucey said. He was thoroughly frightened and sweat beaded his forehead. "*Mon Dieu, nous sommes tout mort!*" he wailed.

Toucey, with considerable alacrity for a fat man, ran to a door at the rear of his office and held it open.

Battles pushed Molly through, then followed her.

Behind him the gunfire grew in intensity and he guessed that at least some of the regular troops of the palace guard had joined the fight.

It was too late for his plan to work. Battles knew that.

But the desire to frustrate Warful and end the slaughter drove him on.

Toucey led the way along a brick-lined hallway with a concrete floor. Here there was no marble and the passageway looked as though it had been crudely constructed as an escape route by one of the old African rulers.

Breaking into a run, gun in hand, Battles headed for the door at the other end of the passage.

Because of a quirk of acoustics, the racketing roar of rifles reverberated through the corridor, overlaid with the sharp splinter of wood and the smash of shattered glass.

The marshal swore. The fight wasn't nearly won, but the fools were already searching for treasure.

The door at the end of the passageway opened onto the rear of the palace.

Ahead of Battles stretched five acres of flat ground, planted with acacia trees and rectangular beds of native flowers. Beyond the trees a grassy slope dipped sharply to a narrow valley crowded with an orderly row of wooden barracks surrounded by outbuildings and cattle pens. The gaudy flag of Eugene de Montijo fluttered over the compound.

The valley was empty of troops, and as near as Battles could tell, the firing had grown less.

All right, at least he could save the survivors, if there were any, from the cages.

A cannon sat to his left, among the trees. Battles ran toward it, but Toucey stepped in his way.

"No!" he yelled. "I won't let you perform this outrage."

There's a time for talking and a time for doing, and right then Battles wasn't in a conversational frame of mind.

He slammed the heavy Chamelot-Delvigne into the side of Toucey's head and the Frenchman dropped without as much as a whimper.

Battles glanced along the cannon barrel and saw that it was sighted as Captain Mabuza had promised.

But Colonel Antoine Blanchard was not to home. He stood in front of the regimental flag-pole and watched the palace through binoculars. Bugles sounded in the French camp and men tumbled out of tents carrying rifles in one hand, buttoning tunics with the other.

Battles grinned, about to put the cat among the pigeons and thoroughly enjoying his act of vandalism.

"Matt, are you sure you know what you're doing?" Molly said, her face worried.

"Nope," Battles said.

He stepped to the side of the cannon to avoid the recoiling wheels and yanked the lanyard.

The cannon roared, jumped, and spat a gout of flame and grains of unburned black powder.

To Battles's joy, the ball flew true and slammed with tremendous violence into the colonel's tent. The tent immediately collapsed in a billow of flapping white canvas, like a monstrous, stricken bird.

Battles let rip with a Rebel yell and turned to Molly, grinning, she would remember later, like a mischievous schoolboy.

"I've done it!" he said. "What a shot!"

The woman nodded. "You've done it all right. They're coming for you and Colonel Blanchard looks like he's foaming at the mouth."

Chapter 51

Vive La France!

Matt Battles looked to the French camp. Troops poured across the border in ordered companies, eagles and battle flags in front of them.

Behind him he heard a shuffle of feet and Marcel Toucey staggered past him, his hands in the air.

"*Vive la France!*" the man yelled, waving as he ran toward the advancing troops. "*Je suis votre ami!*"

Toucey was hit at least a second before Battles heard the rattle of rifle fire.

The Frenchman took a step back, his mouth open, gawking at the unseemly manner of his death. The front of his white suit ran red from at least three or four rounds and he looked at Battles, his face puzzled. Then he pitched forward, dead before he hit the ground.

Bullets kicked up dirt near Battles and others viciously split the air close to Molly.

He saw a company halt and level its rifles for volley fire.

On the run, Battles grabbed the woman's hand and dragged her toward the door to the passageway.

They got inside in the nick of time.

A hail of bullets chipped marble from the rear of the building, thudded into the wooden door, and a few caromed off the left interior wall of the passageway, spraying fragments of brick.

Battles slowed his pace. "Are you hurt?" he asked.

Molly shook her head.

"Now what the hell do we do?" she said.

"The firing from inside the palace has stopped," Battles said. "Either everyone is dead, or Hatfield Warful is the new ruler of Eugene de Montijo."

"I'd put all my chips on the dead," Molly said.

Battles nodded, but said nothing. He led the way to the opposite door, but when he reached his destination he put a forefinger to his lips and made a motion with his other hand, telling Molly to stay where she was.

His revolver up and ready, the marshal opened the door.

The entrance hall was littered with bodies, both black and white, the floor puddled with pools of blood.

It looked to Battles that all the Iron Handmaidens had died here. He saw one woman, no more than eighteen, with her teeth still sunk into Ben Lane's throat and the handle of the man's knife protruding from between her breasts.

At least a dozen soldiers were sprawled in death, bloody testimony to the skill of first-rate gunmen. Fat black flies had already gathered, crusting bodies in a heaving, buzzing mass.

Battles heard the shouts of the approaching French and did a quick count. At least half of Warful's gunmen lay dead on the floor. He presumed the rest, including Warful himself, had died elsewhere.

"Howdy, Matt."

The voice, weak but clear, came from Battles's right. He swung around and found himself looking into the muzzle of Durango's gun.

He brought up his own revolver, his nerves jangling.

Too slow, Matt. Way too slow. . . .

Durango's Colt clicked twice. "Bang! Bang!" the breed said. Then he laughed.

Battles's tunnel vision cleared and the taut fiddle string that was his body relaxed.

Durango sat with his back against a wall, a

couple of dead soldiers at his feet. Beside him Lon Stuart also sat, grinning at Battles.

Both men were wounded, weak, their shirt-fronts stained with blood.

"Where's Warful?" Battles said.

"Hell if I know," Durango said. "Looking for his throne somewhere, I guess."

His hazy eyes focused on Battles. "You were right," he said. "There's no treasure."

"It's a shame so many people had to die proving it," Battles said.

A dozen French soldiers led by a young captain clumped into the reception hall. Rifles trained on Battles and he tossed his revolver away, sending it skittering across the marble floor.

"I arrest you for treasonous rebellion against the French nation," he said in English.

Suddenly Molly was at Battles's side. "No, Captain Mercier," the woman said. "You don't understand. He—"

"Silence, Madame Poteet," the officer snapped. "Unless you wish to share his fate."

"But—"

"Take her away from here," Mercier said to one of his men.

Molly was hustled out, still pleading for Battles, but the captain had already moved on. "Sergeant, find the others," he ordered. "Dead or alive, bring them here."

The sergeant led a clattering squad upstairs and

then Battles was ordered to sit against the wall with Durango and Stuart.

"What do you think they'll do to us?" the breed said.

"My guess would be a firing squad," Battles said.

"Well, that's better than hanging," Durango said. "I never did cotton to being hung."

"Can they do that, execute American citizens?" Stuart said.

"Yeah," Battles said. "If we're on French soil in Africa, they can."

Stuart turned and looked at Durango. "You ever kill a Frenchman?"

Durango shook his head. "Nah, can't say as I have." He stared at Battles. "How about you?"

Battles shook his head.

"The only furriner you ever shot was a poor Swede boy, ain't that right, Matt?" Durango said.

Battles could have denied it, now that it was over and he'd failed on all counts, but he said only: "That's what they say."

"I never shot a poor Swede boy neither," Stuart said. "Maybe I took a pot at one, but I don't recollect."

A small, dark officer with the caduceus symbol on his belt buckle had been moving from body to body. Now he stopped in front of Durango and Stuart.

"Where are you men wounded?" he said.

"You a doctor?" Durango said.

"Yes. My name is Major Solomon."

"Then take a look-see for your own self, Doc," Durango said. "How the hell do I know where I've been hit?"

The major examined both men, then said: "You each have bullets inside you. I will have to remove them later."

Stuart grinned. "Don't make much sense, Doc, digging bullets out of a man you're gonna shoot."

Solomon's face stiffened. "Monsieur, the French army does not execute wounded men. We will nurse you back to health and then shoot you."

"Real nice of you, Doc," Battles said, his tone as dry as mummy dust.

The Frenchman's expression didn't change.

"Yes, I know," he said. "We French are a considerate people."

Chapter 52

The Jewish Doctor

Hatfield Warful was carried downstairs by two soldiers. With him, both unwounded, were the Texas gunman Joe Dawson and Sam Thorne, a fast-draw killer who notched his Colts.

Dawson and Thorne were taken outside, but

Warful was laid on his back among the dead in the middle of the floor.

Battles saw that the man's left leg was shattered at the knee, white bone splinters showing through raw, red meat.

Solomon picked up his black bag and crossed the floor to Warful. He kneeled beside the grimacing man and examined the bloody knee.

After a while, the major straightened his back and said: "Your knee is shot to pieces. I must amputate the leg, and soon."

"And if you don't?"

"Gangrene will set in very quickly and you'll die."

Warful had been studying the man closely. Now he asked: "What is your name?"

"Major David Solomon. I'm the regimental surgeon and I've performed amputations before. You will suffer little, I promise you."

"You're a Jew?" Warful said.

"Yes, I am."

"Good. All the best doctors are Jews. Save my life, Jew. I'd rather have only five toes than die in this place."

The major seemed taken aback by Warful's "Save my life, Jew," but the look of surprise faded from his face and he told a soldier that he had to find an empty room for surgery. "I must operate right away," he said.

"That won't be necessary, Major."

Colonel Blanchard, a massive, big-bellied man with a heroic mustache and full, muttonchop side whiskers, looked down at Warful with little interest and no pity.

"Who are you?" he demanded.

Warful, suffering now that the initial shock of his wound had worn off, said through clenched teeth: "My name is Hatfield Warful, an honest businessmen from the United States. My lady wife and I were captured by brigands and forced to sail—"

Blanchard, his attention focused on something happening outside, was no longer listening.

He said to Solomon in English, so that Warful could understand: "Patch him up as best you can, Major. I'd rather he stood to face the firing squad, but if not find a chair for him."

"Wait!" Warful yelled, biting back pain. "You don't understand. I was taken by pirates and they threw my lady wife to the sharks. They were after treasure and forced me to . . . forced me to . . ."

Warful's words faded to a whisper, then died on his lips.

Blanchard had already walked away and now stood, huge and terrible, over Battles and the two wounded gunmen.

The colonel turned his head. "Major Solomon!"

The doctor hurried to Blanchard's side, his face worried.

"These two, with the blood on their garments," the colonel said, again using his excellent English. "What ails them?"

"Chest wounds," Solomon said.

"Can they stand?"

"Long enough to be shot. Yes."

"And him?" pointing at Battles.

"He's not wounded, sir."

"Then all three will face the guns."

Blanchard smiled at Battles. "I use English so that you're all fully aware of the fate that is about to befall you." He drew himself up to his full, impressive height. "Thus are you blessed by the justice of the French army and its sense of—what do the infernal English call it?—ah yes, fair play."

"You go to hell," Battles said.

"Antoine, please, don't leave in anger."

Blanchard turned and his face registered shock. "Madame Poteet, what are you doing here?"

"I was thrown out by one of your officers, but I managed to elude my guard." Molly stepped beside Battles. "I came here with this man. We tried to stop Hatfield Warful's attack on the palace."

"And the man you call Warful will die for that, never fear," Blanchard said.

"I couldn't stop Warful's men on my own," Battles said, rising to his feet. "That's why I fired on your tent. I couldn't stop the attack, but your regiment could."

"Damn your eyes, man, that warrants a death sentence in itself," the colonel said, his face burning. "You could have killed me."

"We had no other way, Antoine," Molly said. "And even then, we failed to stop the blood-shed."

"What do you want from me, madame?" Blanchard said.

"Release Mr. Battles into my custody."

Molly read the doubt in Blanchard's face and said: "His is a little life, Antoine, hardly worthy of the notice of a great man. As a reward for your mercy, my gratitude would be"—she fluttered her long lashes—"limitless."

The colonel smiled. "Ah, madame, your eyes haunt my sleep at night and each glance you give me invades my tender breast. How can I refuse you anything?"

"Antoine, you are a great soldier with the soul of a poet, a very rare combination," Molly said, throwing back her shoulders and taking a deep breath to better display her considerable charms.

"Yes, indeed, and now that France occupies the port of Eugene de Montijo, we will see much of each other," Blanchard said, his eyes on the deep V of the woman's cleavage.

"And Mr. Battles?"

"As you say, a little life. Take it."

"And the other two, Antoine?" Molly said.

"Beware, madame," the colonel said. "Perhaps you overstep and ask too much."

"I only ask that you spare their lives, nothing more."

"Then I spare them." Blanchard's eyes hardened a little. "Now, no more, and I trust our future relationship will be a bit more profitable for me."

"Depend on it, Antoine," Molly said. "It will be."

Five minutes later Hatfield Warful was carried outside and shot.

Chapter 53

Broken Dreams

"Joe Dawson and Sam Thorne were shot with him," Battles said. "Major Solomon told me that Warful died cursing the Jews."

"And the other men?" Molly said.

"Durango and Lon Stuart? They'll hear their sentences tomorrow."

Battles poured himself another drink. He was a little lit up, and just beginning to feel it.

"I failed at everything I tried," he said, talking more to himself than Molly. "I continually got caught in my own loop, I guess."

"Warful is dead," Molly said. "The slave pens

are empty and all the Arab slavers upped sail and ran for their lives. Don't beat on yourself so much, Matt."

"Things moved too fast for me," Battles said. "Seems I never could slow them down."

He looked at the woman and smiled. "And you, Molly? What about you?"

"I'll go on. I'll survive."

"The Arabs are gone. Who else will leave?"

"Only the trash. Besides, now that Eugene de Montijo is French, I'll have all the paying customers I need."

"Maybe you'll get married?"

"Maybe, but an American woman needs an American husband."

Molly poured Battles another drink, seeing that it was softening him, then a smaller one for herself.

"I want you to stay, Matt," she said.

"Me, an innkeeper?"

"You could do worse."

"Molly, I'm a peace officer. It's all I know. It's all I want to know."

"You'll keep the peace here, at the Saracens Head."

Battles made an effort to hold tight to himself.

"I'm going back to Texas," he said. "Any way I can."

"Well, aren't you going to ask the question?"

"No. All you have to do is give me the answer."

"My life is here," Molly said. "What would I have in Texas?"

"Me. You'd have me. I mean, after all we've gone through together, I've grown to like you. You please me, Molly, like no other woman ever did."

"It's not enough, Matt. Not for me."

Battles said: "We have time. We'll talk about this later."

He knew and Molly knew that later would never come.

"Yes, we will," the woman said.

A sense of loss, of loneliness, of the soon sadness of having to pick up the pieces of a broken dream, twisted inside her like a knife.

That night Battles and Molly lay in a smooth-sheeted bed, both pretending to be asleep, listening to each other breathe, the ghost of what-might-have-been haunting their unquiet thoughts.

Two days later Battles walked to the palace. When guards demanded that he state his business, he replied that he was there to visit the prisoners Durango and Stuart. He was told to wait, and a grinning guard warned that he could be standing in the hot sun for hours.

The iron cages were gone and what was left of Luke Anderson's body now lay in a grave, known only to God and Colonel Blanchard.

Battles was lucky.

His wait didn't extend more than five minutes because Major Solomon was still giving medical attention to the two wounded men and he ushered him inside.

"Both your friends were sentenced to five years of penal servitude on Devil's Island," the major said. "Have you heard of the place?"

Battles said he hadn't.

"Do not expect to see them alive again, monsieur. Many convicts land on Devil's Island. Very few ever leave."

"It wasn't worth it," Battles said. "I mean, for Durango and Stuart and the others. The play wasn't worth the price of admission."

"Dreams of buried treasure seldom come true," Solomon said.

"They had treasure enough in San Francisco, but wanted more. Warful was a convincing speaker and he filled their heads with nonsense."

"Hell has three gates," the major said. "Lust, Anger, and the busiest of all, Greed."

"They didn't shoot you like they did the others, huh?" Stuart said.

He and Durango were confined to a cell in the palace basement, and a massy iron door clanged behind Battles when he entered.

"No," Battles said. "I got lucky, I guess."

"Did you hear our sentence?" Durango asked. "Five years on the rock pile."

"On Devil's Island," Stuart said. He smiled. "I was raised in hell and now I'm headed back to hell. I've come full circle. Now, when you think about it, that's damned funny."

"I came to wish you men good luck," Battles said.

"Wish it, then," Durango said.

"Good luck," Battles said.

"Thanks," Durango said. "Now get the hell out of here."

"Is there anything you need? Tobacco maybe?"

"Only thing I need is tomorrow, and the day after that and the day after that and so on down the line for the next five years," Durango said.

"I don't like you, Durango," Battles said. "But what you're facing I wouldn't wish on any man."

"Get out of here, Matt," the breed said. "I'm getting mighty tired of looking at your long face."

Battles said to Stuart: "Good luck, again."

The Texan smiled, showing his teeth. "There is something you can do for me."

"Anything I can."

"If you get back to the U.S., pick up my horse in Santa Fe. I set store by that sorrel, so keep him for me . . . until I . . . until whenever."

Battles nodded. "You can depend on it."

"Good. Now beat it. You always did talk too much, Battles."

The marshal glanced from one man to the other, their eyes fixed on him, but not seeing him, as lifeless as the painted eyes of china dolls.

"Good luck," Battles said again.

He walked to the door, banged on the iron for the guard, and it creaked open for him.

"Don't forget the horse, Marshal," Lon Stuart called after him.

Chapter 54

The Last Good-bye

"They did all their moaning and screaming at night," Captain Miles Adams said. "Real strange not to hear it now."

"Better the silence, I think," Battles said.

"Strange thing is, when they were packed in the slave boat like herrings in a barrel, they never made a sound," Adams said.

He turned down the corners of his mouth. "Maybe they were too scared to holler."

"Those days are over now," Battles said.

"Could be," Adams said. "But who can trust the French?"

The captain poured Battles a rum. His cabin was hot from the noonday sun, and the air smelled of the spices, ivory, and sandalwood in the hold.

"I guess Molly told you that this schooner is bound for New York Town?" he said.

"It's close enough," Battles said. "And I don't have to go around the Horn again. And meet that damned Argentine frigate."

"The Argies haze you, huh?"

"Took pots at the *Lila* with their cannon."

"They will do that if they think there's cargo on board worth confiscating."

Adams poured more rum for both of them.

"When you reach New York, you can catch a train for Texas," he said. "But that takes money, riding the train."

"Yeah, I know."

"Molly paid your fare," Adams said. He leaned forward across his desk. "I took you on as a favor to Molly, but the truth is I need seamen, not passengers."

The captain was a big man with a bruiser's broken-nosed face, but his blue eyes twinkled with good humor.

"Here's a go," he said. "Suppose you work your passage? You can keep the fare money and I'll pay you seaman's wages for the duration of the voyage."

Battles smiled, sipped his rum.

"I'm not much of a sailor," he said.

"Me and my first mate will show you the ropes," Adams said. "We'll make a topman of you in no time."

Battles didn't have to think twice about the captain's proposal.

"It's a deal," he said. "I surely need the wages."

"Then welcome to the *Shenandoah*."

Adams looked over Battles from his hat, then,

bending over to look under the table, his boots.

"You can't work in them cowboy duds," he said. "Outfit yourself from the slop chest," he said. "Somebody will show you what you need."

Battles felt a subtle change in Adams's tone, a shift from captain and passenger to captain and crewman.

He rose to his feet.

"Thank you for the opportunity, sir," he said. "I won't let you down."

Adams smiled. "I know you won't. You come highly recommended."

He pretended to busy himself with a paper on his desk.

"We sail with the tide, but you've got time to say good-bye to Molly. I understand she's grieving something fierce."

"I'll miss you, Matt," Molly said. "I've only known you a short while, but sometimes a week or two can seem like forever."

"I'll miss you too, Molly," Battles said, meaning it. "I'll miss you in the day and at night. Especially at night, hearing you breathe while you're asleep. It's a woman sound and it soothes a man."

He stepped across the floor and looked out the parlor window.

"I sail with the tide." He grinned. "Hell, listen to me, I sound like an old salt already."

Battles turned, faced the woman again.

"Please come with me, Molly," he said. "We can get married on the boat. Captains can do that, I'm told."

Molly shook her head. "Nothing's changed from the last time we spoke, Matt. I can't leave with you."

"Can't or won't?" Battles said.

"Both, I guess," Molly said.

"Would it help any if I said I was sorry?" Battles said.

"Sorry for what? Some things just don't pan out the way we want them to. No, telling me you're sorry won't do any good."

"I'll write," Battles said. "Send you the money I owe you."

"There's no need," Molly said.

"But still, I'll send it."

A silence stretched between them; then Battles said: "Our talking is all done, isn't it?"

The woman nodded. "Every word. Seems like."

"Maybe you'll come to Texas one day. To El Paso, maybe. In the spring when it's green."

"Maybe one day. When I'm old."

"You'll never be old."

"Then, maybe one day."

Molly looked at Battles. "You'd better go, Matt. Captain Adams won't wait for you."

"I have to go back. You understand that, don't you?"

"You've made your decision and shaped your

destiny, Matt," Molly said. She held out her hand. "Good luck. In all you do."

Battles took it. "And you too, Molly."

"Take care of yourself, Matt Battles."

"Yes, and you do the same."

Battles walked out of the Saracens Head for what would be the last time in his life.

The good ship *Shenandoah* lay at the dock and her captain was already on the quarterdeck.

Afterword

Matt Battles spent two months on the *Shenandoah* and to his surprise found he had a natural affinity for the sailor's life.

Captain Adams told him he was the best topman he'd ever sailed with and begged him to accept a mate's berth, but Battles refused.

"Well, if you ever change your mind and want to sign up for a trip back to Eugene de Montijo . . ."

"I'll be sure to let you know," Battles said.

He had enough money to ride the cushions from New York to Santa Fe, where he got Lon Stuart's horse out of hock.

That the livery stable owner needed a little persuasion of the work-hardened-fist kind to release the animal was convincing proof to the marshal that he had indeed returned to civilization.

He bought a Colt revolver, a secondhand and much-worn Winchester, and lit a shuck for Texas.

Seeing El Paso again after such a long absence brought a lump to Battles's throat.

It was good to be home again.

Battles sent wires to Washington, to his superiors in Fort Smith, and to Governor Roberts, informing them of his return to the fold.

After a month, he still awaited an answer.

"You bought a beer, Marshal," the Acme Saloon bartender said. "That qualifies you for a free lunch."

Battles smiled and picked up his mug. "How long have I been nursing this?"

"About an hour, I reckon."

"It's warm. The beer, I mean."

"Cost you another nickel for a cold one," the bartender said.

"I guess I'll nurse it for a spell longer."

"Still heard nothing, huh?"

"Not a word."

"You can't trust politicians, I say. Even the president. Bunch of crooks, if you ask me."

The bartender wiped the bar with a towel.

"You take my cousin, now, or was he my second cousin? Hell, I can't recollect, but it don't matter. Thing is, he was hung for a chicken thief up Missouri way, and it was politicians that done it.

The mayor and the sheriff and them. Yep, politicians every last one of them."

"Hard way to go, for a few chickens," Battles said.

"That's the attitude I took when I got the news," the bartender said. "I wrote a letter telling the mayor that my cousin was true blue and a Mason. Not that it done any good. They strung him up anyway."

Outside it was dry hot and dust devils did their dervish dance in the street. A huge railroad clock above the bar ticked seconds into the room, and an early-bird saloon girl picked her way through the opening bars of a Chopin étude on an out-of-tune piano.

Earlier the girl had cast a speculative glance on Battles, but her experienced eye pegged him as just another down-on-his-luck drifter and she ignored him.

"Hung for stealing chickens," Battles said. "Well, my, my."

"Yep, chickens it was."

Pleased at Battles's sympathy and interest, the bartender refilled his glass and set it down in front of him without comment.

"Araucanas," the bartender said.

"Huh?" Battles said.

"The breed of chicken my cousin, or second cousin, stole. They was called Araucanas," the bartender said.

"Well, you don't say," Battles said.

"Good chickens, the Araucanas," the bartender said.

"Ain't worth dying for, though," Battles said.

"I know. Damned politicians," the bartender said.

Three men stepped into the saloon, slapping off trail dust from their canvas slickers.

They were all tall men with big mustaches and unfriendly eyes. They wore holstered Colts, belted high where they'd be handy on a horse, and one of them carried a ten-gauge Greener.

"What can I get for you boys?" the bartender said.

The men ignored him.

All three stared hard at Battles and he figured if this came down to a fight, he didn't care for the odds.

"You Matt Battles?" the man with the shotgun asked.

"Who wants to know?" Battles said.

"Jim Baxter, Texas Rangers."

"You have word for me?" Battles said, brightening.

"You Matt Battles?" Baxter repeated.

"Yes, I'm Deputy United States Marshal Matt Battles."

The shotgun came up fast and the other two whipped out their Colts with considerable speed.

"Battles, I'm arresting you for robbing the Cattlemen's and Mercantile Bank in Pecos Station and killing a teller—"

"A poor Swede boy," another man said.

"And for the murder of a posse member and the wounding of two others."

Matt Battles laid his glass on the bar.

"Oh, hell," he said.

Center Point Large Print
600 Brooks Road / PO Box 1
Thorndike ME 04986-0001 USA

(207) 568-3717

US & Canada:
1 800 929-9108
www.centerpointlargeprint.com